PRAYERS of a FEATHER

TZVI PECKAR THE THIRD

ISBN: 978-1-7326066-9-2

DEDICATION

To everyone who has had or has a Mother and to those in the near future who may be born without a biological human Mother.

CONTENTS

ACKNOWLEDGMENTS

My own Mother has instilled the prolific nature of telling the tales that come to my mind. Through her love of reading and fiction, it is my work that is her reflection of passion within me. I love you Mom, I love how you have always asked me, "Are you writing?"

"Oh yes I am; I most certainly am."

1 HOME WITHOUT THE HOLIDAYS

If you've ever had a Mom, you'd understand that you mean the world to them, or not. It's the only way I can explain my relationship with my mom. She's, my Mom. A Mom of me, the middle daughter of a family of four. Two girls to the left and to the right of me, Marigold, and after Suedeo, young Bradley.

"Enough already," I stopped her begging. It was never begging. She didn't beg. Begging was for dogs. My mother was no dog. My mother was a lioness. "When have I missed Thanksgiving?"

"Your brother got stuck in Guatemala that one year."

"No, Bradley got drunk in Guatemala."

"Don't talk that way about your brother."

"Mom," I plead with her denial of reality.

"Yes?"

"Never mind. Did you get my package?"

"The gift card? But you know they don't take those at the Church resale?"

"I know Mom. Buy yourself something nice for a change."

"I gave it to Marigold. She likes to go shopping."

"Mom!"

"Dear, what was I to do with it?"

"It was your birthday present, not hers."

"You know all I want for my birthdays are my children in my heart."

"Mom," I've been hearing that bullshit forever.

"There is a safety deposit box key in my dresser drawer."

"Mom."

+

The workload is ever piling up. The team cannot keep the entry staff on staff for longer than a few months at a time since the pandemic. I do the job of three interns on top of my own. Sick of it really. Ready to quit myself, but then what do I do? Insurance Agencies are steady. Columbus is a place where steady is good. I like steady. Steady is as steady goes. I do like this new stay at home hours thing. That's a plus. But that came with caveats. That too came with a few extra hours. Drifted hours into the weekend. You know the ones you let go on Weds to not get up early, or the extra early ones you took off Tues and then again on Thurs to meet up with some pals at the bar. Freedom and then you're catching up on the weekend and missing the better nights out. So be it.

+

Dinner was Thankful.

"Love you."

"Love you."

"Love you."

"Love you."

"Love you."

The whole nine yards of it. A harmonious enough meal. So we all made the best of getting out quickly. Say our love good byes before Mom screwed it all up. It was instinct. We all moved in unison. Together we went for our coats, our purses, our goodbyes. Mom had no chance. "Love you."

Until Christmas…

"What?"
"Mom fell down," Marigold says over the phone.

"We all just left? What was she doing?"
"She was stepping out to wave goodbye to you all."
"Oh for Christ's sake."
"Don't swear," she corrects me, as they always do, "You need to call her."
"Of course I'll call her. Where is she now?"
"We're at the ER," she tells me, she informs me, however it is not informing me, she is nearly scolding me for not already knowing for not having already called. How the fuck would I know? They always act like that. Something happens and like God's supposed to have sent you a telegram with all the details telepathically if it happened when you were not in the fucking room, and then she actually says, "Can you make it back?"
"What? No, I'm, what do you think?"
"When do you think you might be able to come?"
"I don't know, in a week, maybe two. Shit. Sorry, this is really bad timing."
"For you or for Mom?"
"Obviously this isn't any good for Mom, Marigold, don't turn this into something it's not, you know what I mean."
"I don't think I do. What do you mean? You don't want to care for your Mother, our Mother?"
"I'm not doing this. I'll talk to my boss and see what they'll let me do. Can I talk to her?"
"Mom?"
"Yes, Mom," see what I'm talking about; truly unreasonable people.
"She's being x-rayed. I'll call you when she's out of x-ray."

"Don't do that, it's already 1am."
"I'm all alone here."
"Seudeo lives like 20 minutes from you both. What are you talking about?"
"She has to be at work in the morning."
"So do I."
"But you work from home."

+

I answer. "How's she doing?"
"Not good."
"Oh, that's not what I wanted to hear."
"The x-rays are really bad."
"Are you crying?"
"Come home."

+

"Hey Mom, how you feeling?"
"I'm in terrible pain. Terrible."
"Didn't they give you something for it?"
"It still hurts, dear. Everything hurts. I wish you were here."
"Oh, Mom, I love you. I'm so sorry this happened to you."
"When will I see you?"
"Soon, Mom. I'm coming back soon."
"I'm in the hospital."
"I know, Mom."
"I'm scared."
"I know, Mom."
Seudeuo takes the phone from her. "Ell?"
"Seudeuo? I thought you have work in the morning?"
"I do, but I couldn't leave Mom alone in the hospital."
"She's not alone, Marigold brought her there."

"I know, she's with me right now. When are you coming?"

+

I filed my request for my time off immediately after getting off the phone with them all. A 3am email should give my employer the motivation needed to see the urgency in my need for an absence. By the time I got out of the shower and checked my inbox, she had already rejected my request, for the initial date, but did accept my time off for a day later. Annoying. Petty. Everyone is so petty these days. Control is what everyone seems to need since the pandemic. We all require our own destiny. I am not immune to this want, this need, however, I am the one currently, who has no control over any of this as it seems. Like divine intervention into my quaint life. I reply, "Thank you. I will be able to continue my responsibilities from the location. My Mother will be under hospital care, so I will have plenty of time to do most of my most important of tasks."

I know she'll appreciate that. I will regret that. I already do. Ding. Email reply. "Take the time you need."
I do not believe her.

+

Marigold has met me outside the hospital ER. "Is that what you're wearing?" she criticizes my warm-ups. "I drove like 4 hours…and was here like 30 hours ago? And you want me to dress, how?" – "Nice for Mom, maybe?"
"I don't think Mom cares about what I wear and will be plenty happy that I came, okay?"
"You can't go in yet."
"What? Why not?"
"Bradely's visiting with her."

"So?"

"Only a couple visitors at a time. You have to wait until he comes out. It's fine. You can go home and change."

"You're kidding, right?"

"I don't have the patience to joke with you right now. This is not how I wanted to spend my post-Thanksgiving," she tells me. Like I had less important things to do. "What plans did she mess up for you?"

"Here's Mom's keys. Don't take forever," are her instructions.

"Why, because Bradely's in a rush to go sight-seeing?"

+

Mom's house is creepy with her in it, even creepier without her in it. I don't like it. I don't like that all the photos of us are from before we were in college. Nothing since. A wedding photo, sure, but that's not what Mom thinks about. She only likes to remember us under her web. She likes the roof over our heads.

This isn't the same old house that we all grew up in. We ruined that house. By the time we all got out of there it was a ruin. Dad had sold it and moved into this place a few years after Bradely moved away. Went through six dogs in that original house. Three to natural causes, three to the stupid road. This house never had a dog. Mom doesn't like dogs. Dad didn't care for them either. Marigold was the one that liked the dogs.

Staring into Mom's bedroom mirror I confess, I wanted to be gay, just to piss you both off. I fucked three girls in high school just to make it a reality, but whatever, it didn't stick and you never found out so it was kind of all for nothing. I don't think it would have bothered you as much as when you thought Bradely was gay. That was a real problem. That was a tragedy waiting to happen. I would have been a side-issue in comparison. Change my clothes for Mom in the ER. These people really are not my family. They can't be. They're just so insane.

+

"How are you, Mom?" I've finally gotten inside to see her.

"I've been better."

"Slipped on the ice, huh?"

"I don't know how it happened."

"Mom, it happens; it's ice."

"Doesn't happen to me."

"You were just, not paying attention. Didn't want Thanksgiving to end, that's all, just a mistake."

"Did you have to cancel work?"

"Mom, its nothing," I lie to please her.

"I hate when you go out of your way for me."

"Mom."

"Will you stay the night?"

"I'm gonna be here for a while, Mom. Love you."

"You're a good daughter."

+

Suedeo's waking us all up at 4am that same morning. Chaos has brought scorn upon this family. Her house is on fire. The entire home up in flames. The family is safe outside across the street. She has called and texted us all. I'll let them all in in about an hour from now, maybe two. Not sure exactly how long it will take for them to put out the fire. They shouldn't let the kids watch the whole thing. They will though. They're that way. Violence on TV, bad. Violence in real life, God's way.

+

"I'm so sorry," I tell my sister as she enters Mom's house, her entire family following in behind her. Suedeo looks right into my soul, "We were blessed, look, we're all here, safe, together." I won't ruin that for her. I hug her. She doesn't want the hug. Pulls back. "I'm not upset. Don't treat me like that," she scolds me, "Oh ye of little faith. I'm so very tired. I think we'll take Mother's room tonight."

+

Mom sits up in her hospital bed. To be more specific she mechanically rises her bed to a more upright position. "Lord have mercy, have you heard from Bradley?"

"Why would I have heard from Brad-boy? His house didn't burn down?"

"Because either the Devil is after us all, or God is bringing the family back together."

"This family was never apart, Ma."

"You've been living out of state for years now. And Bradley," she starts, but I can't listen to this shit again, not now.

"Oh Mom, this is neither the place or the time to talk about us growing up and getting our own lives."

"Is that what you call it?"

"Oh my god."

"Don't swear at me," she takes it personally.

"I'm not swearing at you, I'm swearing at the whole god-damn situation."

"You can leave now," she says, stern, harsh, cold, solid.

"Mom."

"We're done. Goodbye."

"Mom, I'm sorry."

"No. Goodbye. Jesus has a plan for you. I don't know what it is, but it is not being here right now. Goodbye," and this time the bed motorizes down.

By the time I get back home, I mean, by the time I get back to Mom's house, the whole team is there and for fuck's sake they're all waiting for me on the front lawn. I pull up to the curb. The driveway's full of their mini-vans. I'm not moving. I'm looking at them all out of the side of my eye. Suedeo and her hubby Darrell. Their rug rats Tammy and Tommy. Marigold and her husband Rick the Rick with their one little mut of a pup kid Bobby and sitting on the porch step, Bradley. Don't curse in front of Mom. Just don't do that. Dumb, dumb, dumb. I get out of the car, make my way slow mo around my stupid automobile, up the lawn, kill a few bugs along the way to face my makers...

"What did you say to Mom?" Marigold is the first at bat.

"Nothing."

"That's a lie," Suedeo knows, they all know.
"If you know, they why do you ask?"
"If you know we know, then why lie?"
"I said what I said, then I apologized. What now?"
"What now?"
I show my palms. I have no clue. I really don't know what they expect from me.
"I don't think you should go back to Chicago," Marigold voluntarily recommends her opinion on my life.
"Okay, whatever," I say and walk past them.
"Where are you going?" Suedeo yells at my back. I turn.
"Inside?"
"I don't think so, we're not done."
"Not done? What are you talking about? Not done with what? You gonna tell me how to live my life some more? You gonna tell me I can't go home, can't go inside, can't say this, can't fuck that? Fuck you, sis," I lose it, "and you too, standing beside them. Some brother you are." And then Suedeo's cell rings, it's the hospital, there is a problem…
+

Everyone's piled into their own cars. Bradly's opted for Marigold's ride. I don't want that traitor riding shotgun. So it's a caravan to the hospital. Now this isn't your average caravan of concerned family members heading to a hospital, no. This is a family of the lord, for the lord, protected, and guided by the lord. There are no seatbelts worn in this family. There is no blinkers used to turn left, right, or much concern for slowing for yellows or obscured vision as long as the obscured object is that of the lord, be it a cross, or one of the brats showing a bible verse from their "car bible." As for me, it was The Cure on eleven with a seatbelt, full coverage, and fuck that asshole in the semi going 55 in 35 residential signal, cutting a red, sending me and my stupid bent block of metal down half a block before pressing us against a set of parked cars.

Mom had fallen out of her bed thinking she was ready to walk on her own, and with that pulled her IV and a number of things followed which led to an emergency which is what we were all responding to. In hindsight it was pretty petty shit considering I can't even speak anymore. No larynx. Amazing I got much of a throat left. No legs. They got completely smashed in the immediate collision. I manage with one functional lung and sustain myself on a diet of tubed foods. My mind is completely in tack and my right hand is fully functional and able to type. Ever since the blessing I have relocated from Chicago to Mom's house permanently with the rest of my siblings who have decided that due to the circumstances it best we stick it all through together, no matter how hard I make it for them to keep myself from burning in hell every single day as my novels of an abhorrent nature slay as best sellers. Sorry Mom. Prayers of feather.

END OF DEATH

He wasn't a man that prayed. He wasn't the kind of man that seeked much of anything. His aspirations were based on the daily needs of sustenance and a roof over his head. He did not travel. Stuck to his small town, his small grocery, his small library, his small, uneventful life. Even love was what came around, not a path to follow, or find. The girls could find him, if they wanted. Ambella was the most recent of the girls. Recent as in three years. But it wasn't until a month ago, that he found himself making a prayer, a wish, a kind of hope as he watched his brand, new baby boy breathing in his crib. "If only things did not have to die. I would care for you forever if there was no death to take me away. If only." If only I understood the grimace of an infant's face. Why does my son squeeze his face when he sleeps? Why does he scrunch his nose? How does he scrunch his nose?

+

One foot forward, like that; I tell my son as I lift his foot and place it back on the ground. He has no idea what I am talking about. He is consumed with giggles and a good couple tugs of Papa's hair. Don't. Come on Ceasar, you can do it. One foot up. One foot down. One foot up—One foot down, but he falls on his behind and I'm frustrated. I give up. Let him crawl. Let them all crawl!

+

Is it terrible to take a two-year-old to his mother's grave? Does this define him? He does not seem to sense the gravity of the situation. This is for the best. Let him run upon the graves and pull the flowers from the dead. Let him spread the dead flowers over all the dead graves. "No!" I holler at him when he starts digging his fingers into the ground of a recently buried man, woman, or child. Child. The small frame with an empty pot of flowers is beside the mound of dirt. I pull Ceasar from the soil. He is filthy. Needs a bath when we get home. Baths are the worst with this one. "You're filthy," I scold him as I let his hand go and replace the flowers he tried to bury in the dirt. The flowers are all fucked up. This is pointless. I hide them in some bushes as we exit the graveyard. Maybe he shouldn't come here with me?

I've gone through sitter after sitter. Single Dad's are a threat. We're either going to fall in love with them, or unable to pay their rate after a couple of good months. As for them, they're either looking for a weekend every few weeks, a full-time nanny job, a place to crash, steal from you, or milk you for everything, and or make you fall in love with them so they can milk you for everything, or, they're just flakes.

Now that Ceasar's three and I really need to get back to work, work. Like full-time. Maternity leave killed me all these years. My State's not the most generous to single Dads, either with a living Mama somewhere else, or a dead Mama like my past-wife. A kind woman. A willing soul to make someone like me feel a little less loathsome with himself. Good person. Not terribly interesting, not gorgeous, and a little bit plain. She was just my type. Did we want to get married? Not necessarily. Did we get married? Yeah, why the fuck not, it won't last. And it didn't.

+

There is nothing at this job that is trying in the least. Thank God for that. I come in, I sit at my cubicle, I type up new forms based on old forms that someone has re-configured, and it is my job to type them in. They say ai is going to replace all these jobs. I don't disbelieve it; however I think some of these smaller businesses will never figure it out and rather someone willing to do it, do it for them. I'm that guy right now, and I love this job. I could do this forever until Ceasar's out of college. Wow, college is going to be a cost. State schools are tough these days. Move to a State with better funds for the kiddos to go to community college first. Get himself a scholarship then, if he doesn't get one by Junior Year. Will he be a good student? Without a mother? Will there be time enough to assist him with that one problem, that essay, the test that's coming up next month, and if he flunks, we're stuck together forever in our apartment. I can't move. I'd lose this job. Any State willing to give community college for free is a State that is not looking for folks like me to fill in a form for them. Chat it up robots -- and Ceasar…you're only five, but I need you to start to focus on your future.

+

Dating sites. Where does one begin with the depressing notion that if social media wasn't a confidence killer, then maybe Dating sites would be a place where people genuinely want to meet people, not rate them, or "not" rate them. I have found to be rated low is an uncomfortable moment while doing your morning business. What I find most disturbing about the whole system is that for some reason, a reason I am sure has been researched inside and out, and used against us and to the corporation's advantage, however, the disturbing part is that when someone you want to "rate" you, actually "doesn't rate" you. Does not give a thumbs up, down, cherry emoji— not even a shrug. They are deep in the emoji menu, so if they're just willing to throw it all to the wind and just see what sticks, then they are not digging that deeply. Those non-reciprocal reactions or non-actions; those are the ones that keep the bowels from bowling and the constipation throughout the days as you consistently check to see if she might have reacted in the last thirty minutes or couple hours. Depends how much attention Ceasar needs at the time. If he's occupied with toys or video games, then I'm usually check the dating app. Yeah, Dad. Way to get out there and get your dance on.

+

Steak and potatoes night. "You're a potato," Ceasar says back to me. "Well, you're mashed potatoes!" I retorted, then tackled the fella to the kitchen floor. It's a wrestling match where you slither along the linoleum. Ceasar will cower after a few swishes around. He's very enthusiastic about physical play for the opening moment. Soon after and he's done. His adrenaline declines and he'd rather stream some old episodes of some old, animated show that I guess kids his age like. I never watched cartoons. My own folks were strict about what programs we could watch. My sister is nothing like me. She's a go-getter. She's out there making her rounds from country to country. Missionary work never tires. Missionary work never ends. That's where I differed from the Pollin family. If it never ends, then it's a futile mission; isn't it? Like prayers. I don't pray. Mom and Dad pray. Adel, my sister, prays with and for everyone. It is rather annoying.

"Get us some forks and napkins," I tell the little guy. I get up. Check on the food. Cooked well. Ready to eat. Just me and my son, my son and me. "Can I cut my steak?" he asks.

"No."

+

I'm bushed. Long day. All red lights home. Frozen pizza for dinner. Math homework. Bickering. I'm tired. "Goodnight little fella," I say to Ceasar from his doorway. "I'm eleven. Never call me that again," says my little brat.

+

History has never been my strong suit. Always struggled with recall. Math makes sense. Science, as a tech, makes sense. Hypothesis and discovery are not for me. I learned code, but we all learned code, and to go onto college to learn more code seemed a little like "discovery," and I stuck to the basics. "Dad, you need to read my paper," Ceasar won't give up. Insists that I am the one to proofread his history paper. "You have a tutor for this," I remind him, yet again. "She can't read this one. I wrote this one about you," he tells me. Am I supposed to be flattered? It's a history paper, not an essay on Single Dad heroics. "Let me see it," and I take the stapled papers from his hand. He watches me as I read each word in his essay on Ancestry. My son has literally made everything up except that he is my son. "What was the assignment?" I ask. "Family history, what do you think it was?"—"Yeah, but none of this is true?"—"My teacher doesn't know that."—"That's not the point."

+

My parents do not visit Ceasar. They mail birthday presents. They do not visit. Last time they came was for his 5th birthday. Balloons, kazoos, orange pop, pizza, and his favorite at the time, strawberry short cake birthday cake. It was disgusting. The kicker was when Ceasar blew out his candles and turned to Grandma to announce, "Hell is for babies." His mother's parents. They too cannot stand to look at him. For different reasons. He barely resembles their daughter. The Mom, grandma invisible, "It's as if everything of her was taken away from us."

I don't put much faith in family.

Would you?

Just me and you kid.

+

No friends at school. No extra-curricular activities. No patience for anything. Not much communication between the both of us. I just pay for what I can, and he just stays invisible as much as he can. Teenagers. When I was a teenager, my parents forced me to do everything I had no intention of choosing for myself. What would I have chosen? I don't know. I've been beaten into such submission that it really doesn't matter what I would have chosen because I am broken and choices are just too difficult to fathom now. I don't even buy the same soap. I buy what I grab in the aisle.

+

My son has left for college. Scholarship. Studying history. He is doing this to spite me. So that we have nothing in common and nothing to talk about. Do you think he'll call? I don't think so. I'll probably see him for Christmas. With his attitude, he wouldn't dare miss a date with Grandma and Grandpa Missionary. Until then, maybe I can focus on these dating sites again. There must be a boring woman out there looking for nothing, but…but what? What do I even want? Been a virgin since my wife passed. That's a long time. Swipe, swipe. Choices.

+

"Happy Birthday to you. Happy Birthday to you. Happy Birthday dear, Grandmaaaaa. Happy Birthday to you," we all sing. Ambella must get the last line in, "And many more!" Ceasar rolls his eyes, shakes his head, and I don't know if I blame him. 120 is old. Does Mom really need to live like this anymore? So many people are living longer these days. I feel old but compared to Ma and Pa I'm still a spring chicken at 92. I don't feel like a spring chicken. I feel like a dried-up raisin. "I'm running for office," Ceasar tells me.

"Why?" I think I heard him correctly, "You're too old."

"I'm, 65, I am not too old."

"You are not 65. You're 72."

"I'm running for office."

"State representative?"

"I'm not going to be a Senator."

"No, you don't have the temperament."

+

"Happy Birthday to you. Happy Birthday to you. Happy Birthday dear, Grandpaaaa. Happy Birthday to you," and I dart my gaze at Ambella, do not. "And many more," she is a monster. Worse in her later years. By 145 she lost all sense of reason. The miracle had come. The lord was amongst us. We were already all in heaven. We are not. We are just all aging without death, or so it seems. I've had nothing better to do than care for my parents. Ambella flies in, trains in, transports in, from more missionary work. She has been reinvigorated with the holy spirit in the last 50 years. "The lord has allowed us more than a lifetime for our words to bring truth to their life. Like your life, Allen. When you see we are blessed, then you too will be blessed."

Ceaser has become a Senator. He had run on reforming the Life appointments of the Supreme Court. He won in a landslide. I did not vote. Felt biased. I know my son. To vote against him would be putting my feelings before democracy. I had only hoped he'd lose. He doesn't. Keeps on winning. Next month they vote him in as leader of the minority, the sixth party in a now heavily saturated party system. My son, the soon to be leader of the Hum Party. A party built upon the non-vote. A party of representatives hell-bent on not voting on bills. They stand for nothing; they stand against everything. A father's work is apparent in my son, a man who seems to relish in the philosophy of indecision. He has gained much with such a path, unlike myself, back home caring for my ailing parents who will not pass, and instead remain shells of themselves with no muscle to pull them up from their beds for the past 60 years.

+

"Go and be gone! Stay and be a burden!" Ceasar proclaimed to the crowd gathered at his latest rally of support. He has gone too far for my taste. A Senator whose only purpose was to sit with his arms crossed has become the Nominee of Hum Party, and under his initial leadership his inaction recruited thousands of thousands of new voters. Voters, who will elect my son, without a thought. It will be the only vote they cast. He has asked this of them. He has insisted, "This vote is the vote that matters. This vote is for all of us, and it is I, Ceasar, who will deliver that vote for our great country that can no longer support the weight of the burden called life."

+

There is nothing to do, anymore. There is an absolute longing for entertainment, yet there is no time for the young to express themselves for our amusement. There is no time for anything but the care of us elders. There are so many elders. We have exceeded 82% of the population. The young are feared to have become completely abstinent. There are a few twists to this lifetime of ours. We live in a state of pure peace, defined by the lack of death. When it first began, when the first generation reached 250 years of age, we entered a dark time, a time where violence reached new levels by all the governments. Ceasar was the first to shoot into the barrel. First one nuke. Wiped out the entire Sudan. Killed no one. Fragments of bodies still wiggling, the eyes of mangled heads pleading for mercy. Even those turned to ash were not decomposing any farther and yes, thinking, as recorded by the Divided Planet Agency. The ash had thoughts, life, a lack of purpose, and a melancholy so wretched and entrapping that even darkness wanted nothing to do with the living ash. And again, and again. Nuke after Nuke soaring through the skies, landing everywhere, dismantling millions upon millions of living beings, even the animals were aging into blobs of life. There is nothing to do anymore.

Ceasar's staff has been caring for myself, grandma, grandpa, and for decades now, Ambella. There's not much left of us to actually care for. Our skin and muscle are as contracted as possible, making for us elders to be basically skeleton with shriveled organs, except for our brains. Our brains just won't shrivel away. We cannot escape ourselves. We all lay here, on the floor. We feed intravenously. We do not need more than sugar water. All of us elders over 175, hopped up on sugar water, except Ceasar the Czars. To rule, lead, manage the non-dying species of the planet, Ceasar and the Czars were sure to covet the remaining technological advancements prior to everyone really needing to care for the generations before them. Technology that apparently keeps them young, fit, and able.

+

They've had enough. The burden was too great. There was no joy or advancement anymore. There was nothing for Ceasar and the Czars to aspire to and do with their fit and able lives. Everyone else was so consumed with living forever that no one could do anything, as I said so many years ago. Ceasar came to me last night. Wanted to talk. It has been at least a century since I last even saw my son. As you can imagine, I was all ears. Couldn't see anymore, couldn't talk. I was all ears. "We're going to move you," he started, "It will hurt, but I assure you, it is for the best." I can hear him pacing around the family. He coughs, clears his throat. I want to ask if he is feeling well. "If you must know, we are moving all the elders, not just you. You won't be alone, not in the least." He's touching me. I can hear his fingers rub along my scalp. "How the youth will handle the move, is much more our concern. Will they suffer from the obvious detachment issues? Or will they rejoice in their freedom? How will they rejoice?" He steps away from me. "It is my hope, yes Grandmother, my hope, that the youth of earth once again procreate, so that we as a species do not sit upon each other, building mountains of useless life that just keeps on living, while my friends and I have nothing left to do. Travesty wouldn't you say, if you could say?"

THE ONLY GIRL IN THE WORLD

She cannot be that interesting. There is no way in Hell that that girl is who he'd prefer. She has no lips, no worthwhile hair line, and from that latex tight pink body suit, she has no personality. I'm leaving. This get together is petty, boring and I really do not need to be here.

"Are you leaving?" the Hostess, who I barely know. Ellen, from boutique. Ellen who sold him the blouse. Ellen who insisted he bring me to this gathering. A gathering of foodies, clothes obsessed fashinovas, gays in the bedroom cutting lines of K, and us, except there is no "Us," never has been and if he lets me leave because of the deflated balloon in pink, then, I'm still alone, like a good percentage of truly valuable people. "It was very nice, but I have an early call time."
"You do look tired."

%

How much did I drink last night? I'm not getting up yet. My head hurts. My neck hurts. That asshole let me leave. Did he even say goodbye? I'm gonna puke.

%

There is nothing to eat here. I gotta go shopping. Nothing. The box of oatmeal, one packet. I'll have a half. I don't want to feel bloated. The calendar on my phone wants me to keep in ship-shape for Barthalamooo. Barthalamoo, will you take me away, off, off to never-never-land, where you won't cheat on me, won't date me once and fuck me nunce. Oh dearest Barthalamoo, you are just gonna be an asshole like the rest. Don't hurt me Barthalamoo. Don't forget that I am yours truly, that I would never deceive you, never break our bond, always, and forever, love you as the one and only. Oh my soon to be Barthalamoo, kiss my lips, hold my hand, treat me like the only girl in the world.

%   %   %

OMG, I cannot get this hair to curl right. Go to the left. LEFT!

"Ugh! Fuck it. You get straight Ms. hair, and you'll love it." I gotta text him. "Running a little behind. Won't be late, but my be right on time." Send. No don't send. "Fuck it. Better to be communicative than a flake."

%

If this one doesn't work out, I'm getting a new cat. Put it off long enough. Miss-ells was my baby, my queen, my everything until Michael, My-cal, like I enjoyed calling him, ran over Miss-ells with the tow. Killed my calico queen with his Jet-Ski tow. Did he tell me? God no. My-call loved me. Couldn't bear to tell me. He just went and fucked my best-friend to get out of a nasty situation. The one where he admits he killed my cat.

I don't come down here that often. It is very gay. The neighborhood is very nice. I always love it down here, just, always feels strange walking alone. A girl, alone, straight in the gay area, always wandering the stores, eating at the restaurants, alone.

%

Big glass doors, several couples wait for their tables. Look for the single guy. Check your phone. You took a screenshot of him. Handsome, 6 out of 11. Is he here yet? No, no. Coming inside? No. That is not him. That is too handsome, holding the door, for his girlfriend? Figures. "Excuse me," I inquire with the Host, "Has Devon arrived yet?"

"Devon? Devon?" the Host, a bleached blonde, with bleached eyebrows, taps down the reservations on his tablet, "Yes," he closes the tablet window, taps his assistant, "Table twelve."

"Follow me," the assistant, a much smaller Asian man, possibly Vietnamese, very flattering as he compliments me as she leads me through the bustling evening restaurant. Not another woman insight save for the handsome man's date, but we've turned the corner to a second, larger room, and I don't have to look at that bitch feeling sorry for myself as I yearn to be the apple of Devon's eye, or that other straight guy in this establishment. I see him. Devon is getting up from his chair. A gentleman. Either good or a cunning fox who'll fuck me if he is actually looking for a conquest. I can be your conquest Barthalamoo. "Anna?"

The charmer assistant places his hand on my lower back and leaves us to enjoy our date. "Hi."

%

He helped me with my chair. I liked it. I can't lie, I really liked it. Don't trust him, that works, for a moment. Will he order me a drink? He hasn't had one yet. "Would you like something to drink," he asks. "Maybe just a glass of wine." "Red or White?" "You choose." "You trust me?" "How can I trust you without seeing you in action?" He raises his hand to catch a waiter's attention. "Good evening," the waiter in black addresses him. "Yes, we'd like a bottle of Pinot." "Very nice," the waiter accepts the request and makes his way to the bar. I've watched him. The waiter. I've watched him meander his way through the crowded restaurant and to the end of the bar. I've watched him passing men as if they did not exist. A man capable of doing his job. A man, who for a reason beyond me, is telling a handsome couple about "me." I know this because they are looking right at me. It is not creepy, or odd. I feel flattered. I feel a little like the only girl here, yet I know in the other room, just beyond the wall, another young lady, who neither met her man here, nor waited on him to arrive, no, a young lady who is the apple of that man's eye, and here I am on a social media first date…

"Have you ever been here before?"
Devon has interrupted my flattery from afar.

"No, have you?"

"Never."

"So, how did you know about it?"

"Searched on my phone."

"What did you search for?"

"Most romantic restaurant to take the only girl in the world?"

"And it picked this place?"

"No, it recommended a dive bar outside of the city."

He's funny. I like that. And he keeps perfect eye contact. Not creepy. A sensitive look. His brown eyes don't lie. He is genuinely interested in me, although we haven't said anything about each other. "Tell me more about you?" He asks. "More?" I'm playing, "What do you know about me already?"

The waiter brings the wine. Pulls the cork, allows Devon to smell it, pours a simple taste in Devon's glass. Devon is pleased. The waiter pours me a full glass and then Devon. I can tell the waiter is not interested in Devon. Devon's not as hot as most of the men this waiter could have in a heartbeat. Probably in the back of the kitchen. Could steal a man from a man. Yet, he cannot pull this Devon from me, not yet, not until Devon falls short, shows his full hand, another let down.

"I know you agreed to dinner."
"Indeed, I did." This guy's still being funny. Is this his M.O? He gonna make a joke out of everything.
"I know you have a warmer interior than you let on."
"Come on. That's a good line, but really, why me?"
"If we knew, then we'd already have met. I thought you were pretty."
"Honesty is sexy."

The waiter has returned. "Would you like to start with anything?" Devon picks up the menu, "Haven't really had a chance…but, how about," he looks at me, right in the eye. This is a moment. I like this guy. Stupid, but I like this guy already. "Cheese plate?"

"Sure. I like cheese."

"We'll take the…"

"Cheese plate. Very good," and he stops, looks at me, smiles. He is looking at my straightened hair. If the waiter likes it, Devon's likes it. I feel good. I feel like-- good for the first time.

"NO!" a loud male voice in the other room. Everyone's startled. Louder than the gibberish of the room, the clink-clink of plates, glasses, forks and knives. "YOU DO NOT GET TO TALK TO ME LIKE THAT!" beat, we cannot hear a response until he really loses it. "I DO EVERYTHING FOR YOU! EVERYTHING!—NO, I WILL NOT SIT DOWN! – NO! DO NOT GET UP!" beat, lots of shuffling from the other room. "NOT YOUR BUSINESS. MANNY! MANNY, WHERE THE FUCK DO YOU THINK YOU'RE GOING!!!"—"NO, GET YOUR HANDS OFF ME—MANNY!"

"HE'S GOT A GUN!" someone yells. The restaurant explodes into pandemonium. Do we run? Where are the exits? Do we hide under the tables? –BANG! BANG!— THUD!—BANG!

Screams!

A busboy rushes in from the other room. Devon has me in his arms under our table.

"Everyone calm down, it's over. It's over," and the waiter looks back behind him, turns back to all of us, "You can, come out now."

People, all men, start rising from under their tables, out from corners, out from the bathrooms they've run too. Everyone is doing their best to pull themselves together. "Come on, we'll go," Devon tells me. Rest-assure little lady, this date has yet begun. So, I think. So, I want. Do I want that? What happened in there? Is there another way out than going through the other room? "I think we have to exit the front," he tells me. He can see I am scared, afraid, torn, and my eyes have melted, and he is correct, inside this scaly reptilian skin of mine, I am warm blooded and so desire to be loved. "I'll lead you. You can keep your eyes closed and we'll go real slow; okay?"

I nod. He takes my hand, helps me up from under the table. He downs the rest of his glass of wine, has not let go of my hand. People among the other tables are confused. Do they leave? Do they pretend nothing happened? Devon is going to save me. Devon leads me towards the break between this room and the horror I may see if I do not close my eyes. Trust Devon, trust he will keep you from the other room.

%

"Did she know him?" – "No, she was seated at a totally different table. I think it was an accident." – "Horrible way to die. Why do that? In public?"

Why did Devon let me hear all that. I didn't see it. Didn't want to hear it. But he led me right through it. Like he wanted to gloat, through all the scared men, that he was caring and saving his princess while they gathered and watched the blood seep onto the concrete floor from the only other female in the entire restaurant. And now blocks away, the woman in what seems this entire neighborhood. "Do you think it was a hate crime?" I ask my dearest Devon. "A marital spat gone very wrong."

"Maybe you should just take me home?"

"Are you sure?"

"We can go out again next weekend. I just…"

"Next week? What about I check on you in a couple of days?"

"That would be nice," and I did kiss him. I didn't think I would, but I was warm, soft, feeling saved, and wanting to reward the favor.

%

He hasn't stopped texting me for hours now. I'm not dead. I'm ignoring you on purpose. I cannot come off needy. I will not be desperate. I kissed you. Hold on.

%

Okay, today I feel lonely. Time to text Devon. "Hi."
"How are you feeling?"
"Better!"
"You want to get coffee, today?"
"You read my mind."

%

That driver was creepy. Kept looking at me in the rearview mirror. I know the difference between a look at the cars behind you and my face. God, this coffeeshop is a cock-fest. Devon sure likes the gay places. "You take me to another gay bar for coffee?" – "This place isn't gay." – "Looks gay." – "You haven't been out since the other night, have you?" – "I work from home. Why do those guys keep looking at us?" – "Jealous?" – "Oh, that's you being funny again." – "Cappuccino, and whatever she wants."

      The barista gives Devon the side-eye. "What would you like?" He addresses me. Stunning eyes. The eyes that look right into your soul. Tingles. Devon's hand has eased onto my lower back. Oh, Devon's jealous. "Do you have Soy?" I ask this barista of my dreams. The barista looks down the line, looks at the few men waiting for their drinks, turns back to me, leans in, looking me right in the...
"Yes, shh. I told them we're out."
"Why?" I ask.
"I saw you in line."

"Okay. Well…"

Devon has pushed himself closer, against me. He is not looking at me and the barista. He is allowing me a private moment yet somehow always assuring the barista I am with him. "Latte, double shot; squirt of vanilla?"

"Squirt of vanilla," he repeats, flirts, gets me going, and won't stop throwing me looks as he prepares our drinks. He is sure to deliver Devon's first, "Sugars are over there," and shoos him off to sweeten his bitter drink; a two-minute window for Barista Barthalamoo and I to get to know each other. "I'd love to paint you," he says to me. "Oh, you paint?" – "Only beautiful women," –clunk—press—clink—switch—the espresso begins to brew, "But not for a long time now." – "Why's that?" – "Lack of inspiration," – Pashhhhhhhhh—PhPhPhPhPh—Clink—He lifts the pour of foam. Delicious foam. His artist's fingers, so delicate the way he has hold of the kettle. Up, down, up, down – "You can paint me."

%

He did not want to let me go today, yet he did, only after exchanging information, and setting a date and a time for this evening. I am such a slut. But Devon hasn't exactly claimed me yet, and besides, Devon may only have been a path to Barthalamoo the Barista. Bradley. Bradley the barista. A barthalamoo that I will let lust overcome us. "Should we enjoy the park?" Devon is quick to ask, consume my time immediately exiting Bradley's coffeeshop. "Oh, how about a little walk with our coffees. See where that leads." – "As you please." – "Too much."

%

OMG, Devon would not let me go. Tried to kiss me three different times along a fifteen-minute walk. Every five fucking minutes, looks me in the eye, leans in. Jesus, it was

too much. I'm gonna fuck Barthalamoo tonight and then give Devon one last chance. He is kinda relationship status, but right now I feel pretty.
%

"Come in, come in," Bradley is happy to see me. Not overtly exuberant, just kind, smiling, happy to show me his gallery, studio of paintings. Naked beautiful women on canvas, stacked upon each other. An orgy of beautiful women paintings, and I was invited here, because for the longest time he had not been inspired. "How many women have you painted?"

"Hundreds."

"You're not joking."

"Exaggerating, to impress you."

"You don't have to impress me. Your art is magnificent. I just," I cannot help but blush, "cannot understand why me? Why do I suddenly inspire you?"

"Rarity is found in the most subtle ways," Bradley explains as he prepares a palate of paint for our session, "For days I had felt as if there was something missing amongst us, men. It was a rabbit hole of sorts. At first, I felt I had seen all the women of the world. From magazines to the television, film, the internet, and even at the coffee shop. Had I seen them all before? Or had I imagined them all before you. And I couldn't shake this thought, this confused moment where so many of my male friends, too were beginning to feel alone, separated from what women want. Cut off from the all, as if they had left us, alone to ourselves, until you were escorted in by him."

"Devon?"

"Is that his name?"

"Yes."

"Are you in love with him?"

"God no."

"So, you are not together?"

"Not together."

"I want to paint you holding a feather. Okay?"

"Only a feather?"

"If you wish," and he slips away, not far, to the tins of brushes, tubes of paint. This is new for me. I never considered posing for a painting, especially a nude. I am so grateful for Devon, for Devon's over-bearing ways. "Where should I go?" – "Here," Bradley hands me a smock, "You can put that on back there." Back in the corner of the studio, behind the red clothed dividers. I feel so, so crazy. Getting undressed in here. With this stranger on the other side. I watch him. He is preparing his palette still. He is so very talented. Me. He's going to paint this? This average body? I trimmed myself nicely though. Attitude. Be a cute little bunny and all will go fine. Am I a cute little bunny? All bunnies are cute. Never really seen an ugly bunny. Yes, that is me, Anna the adorable little bunny, so I put the smock around myself and hop, hop, hop out from behind the dividers. Bradley is no longer by his canvas. He's at his door. He is shooing someone away. "Go!" He turns back to me. "I'm sorry," he steps toward me. I am getting bashful again. He missed the bunny. Who was he so upset at? I feel insecure. Maybe this is all wrong. "I should go," I say. "No, no. That was…nothing, nothing. He won't come back." – "Who is he?" – "The guy next door. Saw you come in. You're okay, he won't come back." – "Why did he?" oh, I get it, "Never mind, I understand. Where do you want me to stand?" – "Here," he says as he leads me by my hand to a stool in the middle of the room. An obvious spot, but it was sweet he led me here. He is very serious. I can see the passion in his eyes as the sounds of brushstrokes along the canvas serenades me.

%

Was the love-making exquisite because we performed for one another, under the gift of art we created together? Or was he just amazing? "I'm in a dream," I whispered into his ear. "Darling, no, it is I who must be in a dream. The only woman in the world has undressed and given herself to me. Darling, dear Anna, it must be I that am in a dream." – "Okay, too much. You don't have to flatter me again." – "Again and always. How else am I to keep you as my very own?" – "What about the other paintings? Where are those loves of your life?" – "Gone, all of them gone. Like a glitch in the matrix, they have vanished forever, leaving the door open for you, the last and forever love of my life." – "Too much." – "Where are you going?" – "I have to work in the morning, love." – "Work from here. I have a computer." – "You're sweet," I say from behind the divider, "I'll be sure to see you soon?" – From over the divider he begs, "But when? I want to make love to you again, now." – "Friday, Hun. I'll come back then." And he follows me to the door. It is his house. "Friday is seven days away. I'll sure to lose you by then."

%

Bradley's got to be on drugs. Nobody has ever been like that. Mental illness, over artist passion, whatever you call it, I am not going back there. Freaky. Falling in love like that, as a man. Too much. I need a balanced guy. "Hey," a stranger says to me as he passes by. No, it is me who is passing him by. He stopped to say hello to me. Weirdo. Ew, and that guy's smiling at me – BUMP! – "Oh, excuse me," I say backing up from the suit. A lawyer probably. Short, a bit stout, and touching me. Why is he touching me? "My god, me?" he's saying, touching my arm, my hand, "Let me take you to lunch?" – "Let go of me." -- "You need to go to lunch with me." – "No, I don't." – "Yes, you do. Out of all of these men, you stopped me. If you didn't want me, then why would you stop me?" – "I don't want you. Now let me go," and I pull myself from his grasp. Another man approaches us. "Excuse me Miss, is this man bothering you?" – "Yes, yes he is." – SMACK!—the guy punches the guy in the face. A sucker punch, hard, cracks the nose, blood splatter; I can't fucking believe it and I've ran…however, he has chosen to run after me? Why is he chasing me?! "Miss! Miss, stop! Let me help you!" –I rush across the red light, just in time to miss the traffic. He is not so lucky. Probably cut off by a bus. Huffing and puffing. I exercise every day. Every day I—huff---exercise—puff—for what? So, I get out of breath after a few blocks? Not even 29 yet? What's gonna happen with me by thirty? Book a car. I don't know if I've always hated this city? A bit uncomfortable. 5 minutes. No creeps around to chase me away. Uncomfortable because it is small. Small in diameter. Small in neighborhoods. Small in selection. Small minded. Suffocating, if you think about it. Everything is designed to feel like the big city. The city of opportunity. The city of men, disciplined, respectable men. A city of suits and ties, shoeshines, and a small trolley train system, unused by the men I want to date. There it is. Red sedan. Wave.

I get in. I looked around beforehand. I wasn't sure, did I want someone to have continued to follow me, or did I want to know someone had not?

"Oh, hello! I'm Daniel, I'm your driver."

He knows where to take me. The app tells him. I don't have to respond. I do not have to even recognize his human existence. One day these car services will be automated and us girls won't have to worry about small talk with a male driver who is always praying to get your interest and fuck you in the back of their red sedan, and as you leave they will lean out their passenger window and recommend, "If you could give me a couple stars it will help my car rating a lot?"

"You work in the city?" the driver asks.
Look at your phone.

"I want to say you look familiar, but these days, I bet you hear that from all the guys?"

All the guys? His dick's hard already. Get me home, please, and shut the fuck up.

"Really dangerous out there for you. What were you doing alone on the street like that?"

"I'm not a call-girl."

"Never said you were. You're the only girl. Doesn't matter if you're a hooker or a terrible lay, you're the only girl in the world."

"I'd like to get out, please."

"We're not at your address yet."

"Not my address. My father's address."

"You still live with your father?"

"I would like you to stop the car, please."

"Anna, it is much too dangerous. I am driving you home and we'll figure out what to do after that."

"After that?" what is he talking about, "STOP THE FUCKING CAR PSYCHO!"--------but he won't! He keeps driving. Faster even. I need out of this car. He's running yellows, now a red! "WHAT THE FUCK!" I yell at him, but he raises his terrible slow-soul music. A car chase, which this is not, but racing along at the same speeds as if the PoPo was on our tail. This music is totally out of place. I am going to strangle him, that will make him stop right? On the count of three. One. Two. Three—I lunge forward, wrap my right arm around his neck and slam him against his headrest. He hits the breaks. I slam forward, knock my head on the headrest. Knocks me dizzy. I'm conscious, but I've let go of him and seeing double. The car door's opening. Holy shit someone, him, the driver drags me by my hair out of the backseat. I'm kicking. I'm trying to break his grasp, but the tug of my hair is̄ so intense I think I'm going to vomit. And—THUD—(she hit her head on the pavement).

%

This is all so unbearable. He had found my wallet. Correct address. He had found my keys. Correct door. He found out very quickly that I did not live with my father. Probably figured out I work, worked, from home. None-the-less, didn't take him more than a few minutes before he raped me unconscious. Meaning, I was still unconscious when he raped me.

He promised to take care of me. Promised to mend my wounds, which he did. Promised not to let anyone hurt me; except him, I guess? Promised to keep our secret. The secret that he's had me held up in my own apartment for over a month now, and I have not had my period.

He insists I never watch the news. He has removed all communication devices. He keeps the windows always covered. The landlord has not bothered to come check why I haven't paid my monthly. He has me spend most of my daylight hours in the closet. I have a single mattress he's mashed in here. I am allowed to use the restroom when he's home. He's usually home. Too scared to go outside, himself. Keeps telling me men have gone ravenous. They are fucking everything that moves out there. Brutal fights in the streets. The military has had to move into the major cities. "Is this even a major city?" I asked when he told me of his sudden return last week after only an hour of grocery fetching. Fetching is what he calls it. Trucks roll through the streets as they throw food to the pitiful human males. Before it was dollar bills and shiny objects that went fast that distracted the male from more war. However, now that I am supposedly the only woman in the world, they have no drive to earn money, no reason to impress others with their shimmering vehicles of seduction, and so, those with left with any sense of decency and value have turned to farming and distributing their fruits and goods freely to the men in the streets just to stop them from raping, and beating upon each other and everything else that walks, or does not walk.

"You're late," he tells me as he opens the closet door. "Mmphh," I say through the bandana he's tied around my mouth, "Mmphh."

He removes the bandana.

"What?" he is annoyed I hadn't waited for him to remove the bandana. He always does. Makes him a gentleman in his eyes. Makes him a fucker in mine.

"I need to use the bathroom," I tell him as I prop myself up. My wrists are rashly from the hours of being tied up. He'll rub ointment on them later. Probably the most uncomfortable routine of his, beside the fact he'd call that routine, "ours." God help me.

He leads me to the bathroom. Correct! Your assumption is spot on. My ankles too are bound so this little princess doesn't slip away from this prince of a Car Driver. Never raped and kidnapped by a … on second thought, everyone's a rapist, even before this. Even I've raped in my day. Eighth grade. Benjamin Michalister. I wanted to know. I saw picts and vids online, but I had not seen nor touched one of my own, in real life. Told him I needed help after school. Met me at the bathroom along the 6th grader hall. "Are you okay?" he asked when he had arrived. "Yeah, I just want to know if you like girls?" – "Sure, I mean, yes." – "Do you like me?" – "Can I be honest?" – "No," I said. Nothing good from someone asking if they can be honest. I pushed him up against the wall, unzipped his pants, dug in there, pulled it out. It was astonishing. I watched it as it grew in my hand. He was red in the face. I held that little thing tight. He wanted to get away, but I wouldn't let him. This was mine. This was hours after school, nobody here, I wanted to see it and see what happens to it. He pushed on me, I tugged on him. He pushed, "Stop it, Anna. I don't want you to," push, tug, tug, "Uh," men can't help but like it once it gets going. Tug, tug, "Stop, stop," push, tug, tug, tug, "Stop!" and that time he really gave me the shove. Pushed a girl. Who does that? Landed on my ass. Laughed when I saw his ding-a-ling half-massed and dribbling the last of his jizz. I was a monster. But this Car Driver right here, this guy is beyond a general monster. This beast is the psychotic side of the devil. A psycho that watches me pee. "You're late," he says again.

"I'm late sometimes."
"No, you're not," he hands me a ply of tp.
"You don't know shit about women, do you?" I wipe, drop the ply, and raise my hands. Oh, you thought he untied me? Wrong. He bends onto a knee and wiggles my panties all the way back up my legs, over the knees, slows along my thighs, all too interested in my skin, as always. I must lift myself off the ring so he can get the elastic under and up my ass, always finishing the job with a little tap, like I did something good. Woof, woof, psycho. He stands up, takes my fingers, so I can balance as I stand up, my skirt falling back over myself. "You're pregnant," he tells me. "I better not be," I am catty about it. I do not want to have this conversation. I am not a believer. "I prayed for this, ya know?" He is getting sappy. WTF? "Ever since our first time together," –please stop reminding me—"I prayed for a daughter." –stop saying that—"A girl, you know, so you aren't alone anymore. And now this," he kisses my hand, "Now the miracle is coming."

%

Unbeatability is a spectrum, a prism depending on your particular if not peculiar, situation. Months ago, it was all so unbearable. The constant dependance on this Car Driver. The LED lights that replaced sunlight for my woken hours. The lack of entertainment. He had removed all the books that spoke even faintly about the opposite sex. There was nothing for this ungodly pregnant woman to do. At first, I sat with my thoughts. Futile way to find peace and happiness. Then I ignored my thoughts. Again, the silence was even more deafening as it laughed at the thoughts that could not be stopped without a bullet and there were no bullets to be found in this apartment. Maybe I should have bought a gun? At least I could swallow the bullet and choke to death. Then I embraced my abductor. I sat with him on the same couch. I put my head on his shoulder. I rubbed him off out of complete boredom. He rapes me with his mouth still. Won't fuck me, I'm with child, but has no problem abusing us both with his fiddling about. I remember him humming, "Three more Months till two for me. Three more Months and we'll be Three!" – Now, now I just am this thing. This thing in the closet. Bloated. Bloated and raw. Bloated and sick. Bloated and with bedsores. Bloated, bedsore, and breaking water weeks early. I'm not going to tell him. I am going to just sit here, turned off, a rape coma, see no evil, feel no evil, think no evil, think nothing, feel nothing, see nothing, hear everything; everything. And the whimpering of this useless male infant kicking and flailing around in my after-birth. Something inside of me figures if I sever the tube, then it might shut the fuck up. He finds us as I'm chewing through the tube. My blood is apparently delicious. I had no idea I tasted so sweet. Like the juice of a cherry with a sour twinge in my jaw. A twinge that reminds me that I am alive, that I have teeth to break free, that I am Mother, and he is weak.

Distracted by that wrinkled meat pile between my thighs, he doesn't have the time to push me aside before my teeth pierce his jugular and rip, tear, sever the man's main artery like the tiger with his prey. No time to watch him die. I must wiggle my way around him, out of the closet, towards the kitchen, so I may find something sharp to cut the rca-cables he's been using to keep me bound for 9 months, maybe 8. Could be 7? I know I was early. The gargling sounds from the bedroom have stopped. I think it's safe to get up. Stand, with the help of the counter. Open a drawer. Empty? Open another drawer. Empty. Drawer—Empty—Drawer—Empty, all of them empty, this whole place, empty. The couch he made us sit on. The piles of Styrofoam noodle cups that he kept me alive with. He had said he stole a truck. No way he did that alone, but he always had noodles for me. Freak. I need something to cut myself free.

I'm at the window. One of my windows. Wow, for the first time in a long time I thought of this place as my place. This is not my place. This has not been my place for a very long time now. I peak out the window. Within' seconds. I couldn't count fast enough. Three guys caught my eye from the street. They're like deer in headlights. One, the burliest of these neanderthals, points at me. I am looking him right in the eye. He is looking past my irises, past my soul, and into the core of all existence. I am in danger.

I close the shade.
and
w a I t.
four, three, two,
am I really the only girl in the world? The door to my apartment shatters into shards of wood. They have broken in. They have found their only girl in the world.

THINGS CHANGE

"Wow, that's so unexpected," she says to me. "What? Did you think I'd wait forever?" I tell her, wave to the waitress. I ordered a coffee, not a coke. The waitress is as mixed up as my ex. "To be honest," she starts, but I'm a whole new man now and I quickly interject, "When have you ever been honest?"

"That's rude."

"I'm sorry, I'm just…I guess you're right. This is all kind of unexpected in hindsight."

"Jerold, I'm happy for you. I really am. I—I'm just surprised. After everything we've been through. Everything I put you through---"

"Everything I put up with," I interject again.

"Exactly! Like, what the fuck was wrong with you? I was a horrible girlfriend."

"You weren't horrible."

"Jerold."

"What?"

"Do you have any idea what was really going on?"

"What do you mean?"

"Come on."

"What?"

The waitress shows up. "Hi, um, I ordered a coffee," I shyly inform her. She looks at me. She's not sure if I'm serious or fucking with her. "He's serious. He's just that way." The waitress nods at my ex, takes the coke and leaves. "Thanks."

"Jerold, I wanted out. That's all I ever wanted."

"I don't understand."

"First year, sure, I was kinda head-over-heels for the shy-guy. The mouse. The cuteness that came with shooting you a sexy eye and your sphincter shooting up your bunghole." I wish she wouldn't talk like that. "Please," I say.

"Jerold…I got stuck. Guilt is a terrible mistress. Once I finally got you, I got scared. I got scared about how much power I had over you, how much control I had over your shy sad, scared little heart."

"I'm not a child, Barbara," I defend myself as the waitress delivers my coffee, "Thank you."

"Of course not, but come on, you were less than, what would you call it?" Barbara has never been good with words.

"Why does any of it matter? Everything's worked out. I didn't think they would, but they did," and I try to sip my coffee, it's too hot, I put it down. She is in shell shock. She really doesn't recognize me in the least.

"This is bullshit. I don't believe you," she says, "Here," and she slides me the tin of cream, "That'll cool it down for you."

"Thanks," and I do pour some cream in my coffee. Blow on it. Take a sip.

"Where did you meet her?"

"At work."

"At work?"

"At work."

"Did you know her when we were still together?"

"No. She got transferred just a few months after."

"Is she prettier than me?"

"I don't know how to answer that?"

"Honestly?"

I sip my coffee. Is Barbara pretty? I've never found Barbara pretty. Barbara has been seductive, kicky, lusty, poignant, vivacious, hale, and if pressed, invidious. She is not asking me the correct question. Months ago. Years ago, now, I would have caved to such manipulation, however, now that the tide has made a turn, I able to see that there are wrong questions, that our teachers were incorrect when they taught us to believe our own bullshit. Barbara believes her own bullshit. "No, she's not as pretty as you." So, I give her a totally incorrect answer in return. Barbara blushes. What an idiot.

"When do I get to meet her?"

"Why would you want to do that?"

"Oh my god, Jerod, I'm not a monster," she lies, "We've known each other forever."

"I didn't think it would be prudent for you two to meet," I tell her. There are things I am not telling her. Things have changed. I am not the Jerod she used to know. I am not a waterspout of information. "Jerod, you have to get over it, whatever it is. I'm not into you anymore. She doesn't have anything to worry about," she lies again. Her eyes seductive. Her eyes wanting to suck anything they can get inside of her. "You want to meet her? And what would you say to her when you met her?"

"I don't know? It's not like that," she touches my hand. She is pitiful and predictable. I sip my coffee, shift my feet so she can't find them for a game of footsy. We're in our early thirties. Awe, she's here. I raise my hand, wave at my beautiful Melony. Melony smiles from across the diner. She has clear white teeth with the kind of smile that spreads past the gums. Her eyes squint tight, her bounty of brown hair covers her shoulders as she scampers her small body down the aisle to our booth.

Melony hops onto the booth and plants a kiss on me. We're cute and Barbara knows it. Melony turns toward Barbara, reaches her small pudgy small-person's hand across the table, "Hi! I'm Melony, you must be Barbara!" Barbara has never shaken the hand of a small-person before. She is unsure, does she take the whole hand, just the fingers…Barbara looks to me for advice, but chooses to take two of Barbara's fingers and make a dainty shake. "We're not in the South, darlin," Melony says about the weird handshake, "You can hold my hand next time," and she takes Barbara's hand into her hand and kisses it, "You're prettier than Jerod let on. Probably didn't want me to get jealous." And she kisses me on the cheek. Barbara smirks, jealous, "Yeah, probably."

"Restroom, hun?" Melony asks me. I show her. It's just down the way. She excuses herself. Barbara waits until she's out of earshot and yet still leans in to ask, "That was so unexpected!"

"I knew you'd say that," I tell her.

"Jerod, she looks just like you."

"What's your point?" that's an uncomfortable thing to say to me. I cup my coffee. A habit of mine to keep my hands occupied, away from hers. She knows my games, she puts her hands around mine. Don't do that. "Why does she look like you and me, Jerod?"

"Why are you touching me, Barbara?"

"I care about, Jerod."

"Do you?"

"Of course I do," she is honest.

"How many times did you cheat on me?"

"What does that have to do with her?"

"Nothing."

"So why are you bringing that back up?"

"Because you are holding my hands."

"I'm worried about you, Jerod. Did you do something you weren't supposed to do?"

I look down towards the restroom. Figure Barbara has about a minute or two left before Melony exits that door. "Not sure what you're asking about," and I slide my coffee towards myself and take a sip. Her hands lay flat on the glittered tabletop and slide back to her side. From the corner of my eye, I can see Melony exiting the restroom door. "Don't worry, it wasn't your egg," I tell her. Melony is getting closer. Barbara mouths the words, "Not my egg?"

"No, just a strand of your hair. I made the egg from that. Cutting edge stuff."

"She's. . ."

"Beautiful."

"Stay away from me, Jerod."

"Oh, Barbara. I don't wish to ever see you again even in death. I have moved on. Come Melony, let's start a family." Barbara runs from us to the restroom. I assume she is feeling ill. Lovesick. But like they say, things change, and you can't go back to the way things were.

NO GAIN, NO PAIN

"I don't want it," I tell him and kick the quarter back at his feet as he walks along. I'm just sitting here eating my half a sandwich. I'm not panhandling. I'm not a beggar. The mayo on this sandwich seems to have turned a little. I might not finish it. I get up, toss the last few bites into the trash and head east.

<0>

The river is calming in the evening. The boat traffic has subsided. The street traffic behind me has subsided. This is where I tend to go to decompress from my day. A number of us, people, do this. I keep my distance from others. Last thing I want to do is come off as asking for something, looking for attention, comradery, anything really. I do not want anything. If I could have my greatest of all wishes, that would be the simplest of all wants, the want of nothing. To obtain, retain, acquire, and/or desire nothing would be nothing less than the…I am not even so sure what that would be, for it would be nothing. Alas, here I am still, with a shirt on my back, pants on my legs, and shoes on my feet welcoming another night of calming sleep ashore the

Detroit River, under the Canadian moon, on the American side.

<0>

Breakfast is a bagel from my find yesterday evening behind the casino lot. Water's always crisp from the fountain. Human body does need water. Shame really. Needs water, air, nourishment of all sorts. That really is earth stuff so it's not a glutton, glamorous, or really anything but existence, so not much an ask as much as a find. Thing about wishes and prayers is they, out of all things, don't seem to come cheap in this society. I see it all the time. Lines of folk gathering to get into the big churches. Have to carry their fancy handbags to carry the money to pay the rent on the services. Very expensive to cast a prayer in these parts. And not just this city. No. I've been to a lot of cities. You don't find water and air sitting in one spot. You have got to keep moving. I'm just here now, and the water is crisp. I like it.

<0>

When I was younger, my thirties/forties, I'd chew the dry ends of my hair to keep it at bay. Past the time. Gave my jaw something to do. Younger still, I would chew gum. Hard to be completely insightful, or reflective, maybe walk the walk, yeah, that's what I mean. Hard to completely walk the walk in your twenties. Life is still so new. You're just beginning to experience pain and hardships. Chewing. Acquiring gum to chew, was something I did. If I did today, I may spend a time with regret, but as I reflect, I wonder, would I have chewed my hair instead? Now I just click my tongue. Much more fun.

The newspaper said they extended this river walk for miles. If so, why now? Was there something missing? Is walking along the water a necessity for survival in this city?

Deeper up there, North, there were a lot of residential streets. Mostly residential. A strange town. Quieter than most. I've walked a lot. Makes you curious about the river walk they extended. Why? Why here? Now? When was it decided? Who decided? – Scooters. Seen those too. Everywhere. Tilted on a tree here, tilted in a bush, tossed in the street, kicked to the curb. Don't work without a credit card. Even back in the day there were pay phones that took coins. Those don't exist anymore. Everyone need a bank or a bank card or a EBT or a Sugar Daddy these days. A Sugar Daddy, Mama who has a card. Not me. No card for me. No need for a scooter or a bicycle. Two feet. That's what God gave me and that's all I got. Crawl if I tire and I'm not home yet. Home. Home is where the heart is. They say the heart wants what the heart wants. Nah. The heart beats. It's the drum of the body. A rhythm in the night. My home's right here, on the left side of my chest. I'm always home.

Pizza box. Couple crusts. Who leaves square crust, crust? I tell ya, out of towners are real strange when they get into this city. Someone told me that once and I didn't believe him. Now, I believe 'em. Whole-heartedly. Out-of-Towners do not know how to Detroit in the D. I gotta cross Woodward. Headed up to 7mile, then gonna go back East, make a long loop back to the river. The unscenic route. Maybe 8 mile, but that might be too glamorous. Lots going on, on 8 mile. Better stick to the lonelier mile.

<0>

Bim-Bam-Biddle-Bee-Bamm: Bim-Bam-Biddle-Bee-Bamm
  : Bim-Bam-Biddle-Bee-Bamm : Bim-Bam-Biddle-Bee-Bamm

Fun, no sun, but fun, with pun, and zun be done. A liquor store. They call them party stores here. A cute term to tame the pain. Always someone walking in. Always someone stumbling out. Some say hello, some walk on by.

A few get in cars as a few stroll with their paper bags. That guy's opening a pack of gum. Unwraps the stick, bends it against his bottom teeth and drops it in. Chew, chew, chew to the car. A truck actually. Rusted truck. Been through the snow. Big tires. "Excuse me," someone says. I must be in their way. I step aside. "No, no. I want to talk to you," he says to me. I point to myself. "Yes, you."

This guy looks extremely sad. Not on the surface. On the surface he has a jolly round face. He's been balding since his early thirties. Now in his mid-fifties he's learned to live with it. He's let the sides grow out to a distinguished length; one and half inches. It's a bit curly. Maybe a wave or two to the inch. Kind eyes, but those are the eyes of the sad. He is deeply sad. He has never seen anything. He has lived a bland life and felt no joy, no sadness, no confusion, no desperation, and this has led him to an abyss that has burrowed so deep behind his eyes that he does the unimaginable and I could not be more sickened and confused myself. "Take this," he says to me as he hands me his lottery ticket. My hand instinctually takes the card. Now in my fingers it belongs to me. I have failed myself. My lifelong ambition has failed. I have accepted a gift, I have acquired something. "I do not want it," I tell him, but it is too late, it is mine. He leaves weeping. All of his sadness pours onto the pavement as he rushes to his sedan, gets in, nearly slips on the ice of his own salty tears, starts his car, looks back into my eyes, reminds me of his gift, and drives off leaving the single lottery ticket in my hand. The lottery ticket I intend to toss into the trash right beside me just as someone has grabbed me by the bicep. "Did, did he really give that to you?"

"Maybe?"

"You're rich. You are filthy rich! Get inside," and he pushes me into the swinging metal door inside the liquor store. Opens the cashier door, gets me inside, behind the protective glass, sits me on a stool. There are patrons pushing up against the glass looking at us. On the TV, which the cashier is raising the volume on, is the re-announcement that there has been a winner and it has been called in from the address…Yes, this one. This liquor store. I look at the lottery ticket. I have never felt more ill, more disgusted, more discouraged; never since the Christ has a man felt more forsaken for his prayers.

0.000<$$$$$$>000.0

"It's not a problem, we'll figure this out."
"Here, fill this out. Doesn't matter what name you choose now. Do try to put the most reasonable birth date and year. Best if you were born here—We're working on the P.O. Box address so leave that blank for the moment."
"Good. Good. Okay, we're still waiting on that address, then we can process and wait for a temporary Social to be processed."
"Do you have a preferred bank?"
"Here is your Temporary Social. Plug that in there. Add this address to this form, then we'll get that bank account set up. Question. Do you want to set up a retirement fund?"

0.000<$$$$$$>000.0

FLASH BULBS—BIGCHECK—DOLLARS—TOOMANYPEOPLE—TVDOLLARS—"May I leave now?"—PUSH THROUGH CROWDS—HANDLERSPUSH—TOACAR—FRONTSEAT—THEYCLOSETHEDOOR—

I am alone in the front seat of this car. A woman with a tablet is tapping on the passenger window. I look around. I do not know how to roll the window down. She points at a button in the middle of the front two seats. I press it. The passenger window rolls down. I release the button. She curls her beige painted fingernails over the edge of the pane, leans her face to the open space. "Do you have somewhere to go?"—"Sure," I tell her—"Good. Enjoy. And congratulations." She steps away. "Wait! Miss?" She comes back to the window. "Yes?"

"What do I do with the car when I'm done?"

"It's your car sir. It's a gift. We knew you didn't have a way to get around, so we got a donation."

"But this is a new car?"

"We couldn't give you a used car? Enjoy, Mr. Potanomonanmo." This time she truly walks away and I am alone with my new car. I press the start engine button and roll out of the drive onto the road and to the river. How do you drive again? Been so very long.

0.000<$$$$$$>000.0

Tap-Tap-Tap. On my window. Wakes me up. Bright light blasts through the pane into my pupil. I cannot help but cover my face. Tap-Tap-Tap with the back of the flashlight. The beam shines back and forth. Terribly discombobulating. I recall the window button in the middle of the seats. I accidentally press the passenger button. This angers the officer. "Sir, I'm going to need you to step out of the car." I roll down the correct window. "No, sir. Step out of the car." This is all so foreign to me. I figure best to do as he says. I open the door. This startles him. He leaps back, pulls his pistol, aims it at me. "Arms up. UP!" I throw my arms up. "Step away from the vehicle." I step away from the vehicle. "Did something…"—"Quiet. Is this your vehicle?" –"Um, I suppose so?"—"What does that mean? Do you own this car or not?" –"They, they just gave it to me."—"Up against the car."

They've got me against the car. I am obedient. They are not arresting me. I do not suppose they are. My hands are not cuffed, however they are being held as I am patted down. I am not carrying anything. He turns me around, his hand on my chest. He does not want me to move. I will not move. My arms are up. Bent at the elbow, palms open, gentle fingers, and doing my best to look him in the eye. "License and registration?" – I am not sure how to answer this question and he knows it. Now I am in trouble. Trouble I am not aware of or been schooled upon prior being caught doing something. "Is this your car?"

"Yes."

"Do you have registration?"

"I. I'm sorry, I do not know."

0.00>$$$$<00.0

He handcuffed me about a half hour ago. Maybe longer. A second PD car is pulling up. Back up. Takes two to put this criminal down. The other cop gets out. Swagger to my cop. They chatter in the road. Cars drive by. Cars cruise by, slow. I watch them cruise by. I don't really know exactly why I'm handcuffed, but I am assuming it has to do with a registration thing. The temporary license is in the glove compartment.

They're gonna search the car. They popped the trunk. Nothing in there except a briefcase of money they gave me at the lottery office. Nah, just kidding. Nothing in there. Nothing anywhere. I don't got shit. Nothing but the clothes on my back and this weird car they gave me. Oh, the bank card in the glove compartment that's worth 55.5 million.

They're checking the glove compartment now. They took my stuff out, walking to their car. What are they doing? Taking forever.

0.00>$$$<00.0

He's handing me the papers he took from my car. I am instinctually taking them with the cuffs still around my wrists. "Oh, my bad. Let me get those off of you." He casually uncuffs me. "You ready to take a sobriety test Mr." he looks back at my license tries to pronounce it correctly, "Potanom-momo?" – "Potanomonanmo, sure. I do not

drink." – "Whatever you say. Over here." –
Do This
Do That
Do This
Dance Like That
Sing Like This
Skat Like That.
Who the fuck are you?
"Hey, come here?" one of the officers calls my cop over. He shows him his phone. He's been watching the internet while I've been grilled for intoxication. "This you?" He shows me his phone. I can't see it. I am assuming they figured it all out now. They look at the phone, look back at me. "Holy shit that is you," they approach me, "You're the guy that won the fucking lottery?"
"Yeah."
"Why didn't you say that in the first place?"
"Why would it matter?"
"Why would it matter? Are you crazy? You're like a zillionaire. Why are you parked by the river?"
"I like the river."
"Man, why didn't you say that when I asked you what you were doing?"
"You never asked me that?"
"This guy."
"Well, do whatever you want. But be careful out here. It's not safe around here. Better to get yourself up to Grosse Pointe, find a nice hotel on the lake. Shit, you can afford to buy a house tonight, haha." He pats me on the back and the cops leave. They just leave. The end. They just leave.

0.00>$$$<00.0

What are the options for a person like me? Really? I wonder this as I do drive up the coast of Lake St. Clair. I curl all the way until Canada and then make my way up the border to Lake Huron. I have decided to drive along the borders, as a motorcycle does in a carnival bowl. The electric car seems to take me very far, hours upon hours. I can sleep and drive some more. So many hours. Maybe I will just leave it be when it runs out of power? It doesn't take gas. That's good. However, I don't see why I would pay for electricity either. Couldn't this car just regenerate that?

0.00>$$$<00.0

I have pulled into a "charging station." The car has not gotten very far in the least. A bit disappointing. One really would think with all the spinning the thing could keep going. "Do you know what I do?" I ask the attendant. "No, never used it. I think you just swipe your card like gas." And the guy's back to tying up the trash to carry it out back to the dumpster. Makes me think I'm hungry. Maybe I'll buy something? First charge the car. I swipe the Bank Card in the charging machine. It asks for my zip code. I type in the PIN the lady had me create. 9022. It doesn't work. I try again. Swipe. Zip code. 9022. Nope doesn't work. I go inside.
"Um, I am trying to charge but my card isn't working."
"Here, how much?"
"All of it? Um, and this, and this," and I hand her a pack of mint gum and a chocolate cookie. She has me swipe and enter my PIN. 9022. It works. Success. "Thank you," I say take my stuff and leave. I eat the cookie right away. I was hungry. Gum. Hmmm, do I really get into this habit again? Has the money already gone to my head? I will wait. Let it sit in my pocket.
I drive North. Up the coast. Up the East Side of the Thumb.

0.00>$$$<00.0

I've parked just off Burnt Cabin Point, the upper most Northern point of the Michigan Thumb. I have walked out here as far as I could go as well. There is nothing here.

Nothing of value to anyone really. Nice and bland, however, a monument known the less. Known to millions. A landmark. A way to give direction to the directionless. Even the thought is as simple as my journey to the end of this dock. No mitten without the thumb. I stick my gum under the railing and wander back to shore as I unwrap yet another stick of gum; a glutton. I want to find an ATM.

0.00>$$$<00.0

All these gas stations have ATMs and bathrooms. Who knew? Swipe, PIN, um, Checking, um, Other Amount, 55,000,000, enter—ERROR $200 MAXIMUM WITHDRAWL—oh. $200. No Receipt. Machine makes sounds, gives me eight $20 bills. I walk up to the cashier.
"Are they all like that?"
"Like what?"
"Only give you two hundred dollars?"
"I don't know, but don't say that out loud man."
"Here," I offer him the two hundred dollars.
"What do you want?"
"Nothing," I earnestly reply.
"Get out of here."
I'm not going to argue with this man. He would just see it as intellectual game play as opposed to honest deliberation. Someone will take this burden out of my pocket. Not the gum. The gum's going to stay in there for a while longer. There is something to be said about a little sin occasionally.

0.00>$$$<00.0

I've pulled over on a turn out by the lake. It has come to my attention the lake is not a public space. There was nowhere to pull over and sit. Everything was a driveway, a house, a dock, a pier, a this, a that, a not for us. This little spot is a callbox spot. I figure I got a few minutes before a cop cruises by. I got my story straight now. Tell him the truth.

Show him my license and registration and tell him the truth. I see, this spot's been a nest for some travelers. Maybe teens. A hotspot to make a small fire, drink a few beers, finish off this bottle of vodka. Gives me an idea. I pull the twenties from my pocket. I roll them, one at a time, and slide them in the empty bottle. "That'll do," I say aloud and toss the bottle into the vast lake. "You can't do that," announces a voice from behind me. I turn. The police officer I knew would come. Come at this moment, that I hadn't timed well. "Oh, I'll go get it," I say, turn, begin to disrobe and enter the water. "Stop. Do not do that. Sir! Get out of the water! Stop! STOP!"

I stop. Turn around. I am calm. I do not understand why he is so agitated. "Arms up," he says. He has his weapon drawn. What is going on? I have stepped out of the water. He doesn't want me to come any closer. "Is that your vehicle parked up there?"

"Yes. I have my license and I have my registration."

"That wasn't my question. Why are you parked here?"

"I wanted to look at the lake."

"But that isn't what you were doing, was it?"

I am not totally clear what he's asking. "The bottle?"

"Is that what it was?"

"What?"

"What were you discarding in the lake?"

"Uh, yes. Yes. It was just an old bottle of vodka that I put money in."

His finger moves on his gun. Did he take the safety off? He did something, something that prepared the gun. Something that matched the clench to his brow, the shiver up my spine. "I'm going to need you to come up to the road. Let's do this slowly, okay. No sudden movements," and he waves the tip of his gun for me to move first. He follows me up the small embankment and through the bushes to my car, his patrol car, and the road.

"Why don't you wait here," he says as he walks my license to his patrol car, I guess to run it like the others. A car is the hinderance I used to imagine it would be. Not even 24 hours and I've found myself losing a lot of quality time. In this particular case I can see the wrongdoing, however, if you actually break it all down there is no wrongdoing at all. While this guy runs through his protocol, I will explain why there was no law broken by me throwing the vodka bottle full of twenty dollar bills into the lake. The bottle is made of glass. Glass is sand. When the glass is bashed against a rock it will shatter. At that point the bills will be released. The bills, made of cloth not paper, will float around until found. At that point they will return to the ever-rotating cash economy. So, all that is happening at this moment is a waste of your tax dollars, and now that I won the lottery, my tax dollars. "Here is a ticket for littering and loitering. Have a good rest of your evening," he says and walks away. Loitering? Not once did he even inquire if my car was in need of service. That was a lot of assumption for one quick interaction.

0.00>$$$<00.0

Public parking lots. These seem like the places worthy of my card. At first thought, I imagined they might be free to the public, however as upon entering, it did require I insert the bank card. I had a nice view of the lake from up here. Definitely unused restate. The most unused. It hadn't crossed my mind until the latest run in with the law, but as I cruised into this lakeside town after their line of beachside hotels, I saw the parking lot, five stories high, and a lightbulb just lit up, ya know. I could sleep in my car there and no cop would tap on my window. If I wake up around eleven, breakfast rush will be over, and I might be able to find someone's leftover waste to put to use before I continue my drive up this coast.

I recline the seat. I electric open the skylight blind. Clear skies tonight. The stars are brilliant. The lake does have a gentle sound. Not the rush of an ocean. A trickle like a far-off stream. There is water; however much water there is, it is not imposing.

--TAP—TAP—TAP—I WAKE UP!

Someone is at my window. I roll it down. I am a car pro now. "What?"

"Are you sleeping here?"

"Yeah, why?"

"You can't sleep here," he tells me.

"Why not?"

"Because you just can't."

"I don't want to drive."

"Are you drunk?"

"No."

"Are you too tired to drive?"

"Yes, that's why I'm sleeping."

"But you can't sleep here."

"Where do you want me to go?"

"A hotel? There's like a zillion all over here."

"I rather not."

"Whatever, you can't sleep here."

And he just waits. He waits for me to do something. I stare forward. I do nothing. I do not sleep. I am not sleeping. He taps on the door. "I know what you're doing. You can't do that either. I think you better go."

He steps back, walks away, all the way to the elevator. Presses the elevator door, waits for the elevator watching me. Watching me. I turn the car on. The elevator comes. He holds the door. I pull out. He watches as I pull around the corner.

0.00>$$$<00.0

Met a rabbi once that told me that King David used to take 60 winks. Maybe it was 80 winks. Could have been 16 winks for all I can remember, but it was a number of "winks." The story has come to mind. A tale that has become of use to me. Drive. Park. Walk. Winks. Drive. Walk. Winks. Walk.

Winks.Walk.Drive.WalkWinkSWalkWinkSWALKWIKSLS
. "Excuse me," I address a young woman down on her luck
outside a laundry. "I ain't got no change," she barks at me.
"I got some," I say. She looks at me. "Come on," and I go
inside the laundry up to the ATM, swipe the card, withdraw
$200, turn to give it to her. She hadn't followed me in. She's
still outside. Still nursing the unlit cigarette butt. Still cursing
at the trashcan. This place is empty. My clothes do smell a
little crusty. They could use a good bath. I make change,
strip down to my underwear, run a wash, and deliver the rest
of the money to the youngster.
"What's this?"
"For you," I tell her.
"I not a trick, homo," she tells me.
"Nah, I'm washing my clothes. That's just for you," and I
give her back the money. She takes it this time. Puts it in her
bra. The pressure pushes her bra out of her already
drooping shirt. She pulls it up. It doesn't help as it droops
back down. I adjust myself and wish her the best, "Don't
spend it all in one place," and I head back in. "Don't tell me
what to do with my money," she scolds me, spits on the
door behind me. The saliva, stained with tan of tobacco
drips down the glass as two police officers take her by the
arm. "Uh oh," I exclaim as I step back, deeper into the
laundromat, hoping not to be seen in my briefs. Maybe I
should duck down. I think they got her for soliciting.
Exactly what she wasn't doing and did not want me to be
doing. They're putting her in the back of their squad car. I
fucked her day up. I gotta get out of here. My clothes are
soaked. Soaked and suds. I got no choice. I put them on,
flop, slop, flop out the door, drip, drip, drip to the car, soak
the seat, gotta buy new clothes, drive to a department store,
but where, where can I, maybe there's a partystore around
that I can get some dry stuff. There! I pull over, into the lot
of a good old fashioned partystore. I drag my wet self in. I
find a bag of white t-shirts, a pair of navy-blue sweatpants
bag of socks and I'm swiping my card, and no questions

from the party store!

In the backseat I'm stripped down to my nuthings. Quick with my sweatpants bottoms. I am not slipping into a misinterpreted indecent exposure arrest. Covered and now the shirt, and I can breathe. Breathe. What do I do now. Eat? Chew some gum. Gum? Awe shit the gum? Ew. The gum got all soggy and suddzy in the pocket. Toss it out the back door. WHOOP WHOOP. You have got to be kidding me. I look up. The cops already there. So fast. Like a ghost. A ninja. His flashlight so bright in my eyes. I cannot help but shade them with my hand, palm out, always palm out. Defenseless. I am defenseless. "Out of the car!" he is demanding from the get go, "Out!" I move, "SLOW! SLOW!" He's so fucking scary, I don't know what to do. My fingers have grasped the metal curb of the passenger floor. I am frozen, however my feet seem to be scurrying, trying to find a footing. "You need to get out of the car," he is drawing his weapon, slowly. Why do you need to do that? I'm complying. I am getting out of the car. "Slow," I'm moving slow. Oh, God, what do they want from me. "Stay on the ground," he orders me. On the ground? Out of the car, on the ground? How on the ground? Like this? I have my knees bent on the ground, my toes bent, my palms flat on the ground, my elbows like a pushup, "NO! ON THE GROUND!" and a foot pushes my back to the asphalt. My stomach hits the asphalt, hard. But it was the pressure of his boot on my back that forced me down. There is a knee on my back. I can't move. It hurts. If I shift a little it'll feel better, like that, yeah, okay, like, OW, what the fuck, oh god that hurts worse. Stop. Come on. Let me just, like, like that, like that, okay, yeah take the call, I can breathe better. AWE! THAT'S MY KIDNEY! OH GOD MY KIDNEY! MOVE MOVE IT GOT TO KICK KICK KICK OH GOD--- BAP!---HIT ME IN THE HEAD…Oh that hurt…but the knee on the spine, just the knee on the spine, stop twisting on the spine. OW THAT BURNT! He scraped his knee off. That burnt. I'm not moving. I don't know what all that was

about, but I'm not moving. Don't even breathe. Breathe a little. Baby breaths. Small baby-breaths.
He's got a wrist, click clack. The other wrist, click clack. Lifting me up. I stay limp. "Get the fuck up," he complains. Okay, work with him. If I don't I'm resisting? Where am I going? The back of the squad car? What I do? Do I ask him? Ow? He hit my head? He did what that fucking asshole president said to do. Fuck this cop. WHOOP WHOOP WHOOOOOO!!!! Where are they taking me? What about the car? I look down at my sweatpants. Oh, I don't have my license, or that registration paper…or the bank card. I got nuthin.

FAST CAR

Everyone but me.
Mustang
Porche
Last Camero
Corvette
Lambo
Ferrari
Fast car. Everyone but me got a fast car.

My Dad said I couldn't get a fast car for my first car. Dad said I should never get a red car for a second car. Dad said never drive drunk and stick to a sedan. Dad gave me his old pick-up to slow me down on the freeway. Dad had never wanted a fast car, never driven a fast car, and until now, never let me even consider a fast car. Dad's dead now. Dad's being dropped in the dirt and I'm looking to the lord for a blessing, a silver lining to this sudden storm cloud, this pain so deep and strong, that only the laughter of me in a fast car could possibly cure a little of the pain.

I said goodbye to my father. A couple steps around the head of the grave and I'm saying hello to Mom. "Enjoy each other again. Dad's missed you, a lot," and I left a small stone on the top of Mom's headstone, Sarah Zapenski, Mother of one, beloved wife, fearlessly independent. And I made my way to my sleek, shiny blue Mini Cooper, and drove off to the wake.

$ $ $

My hand slides around the apple red bespoke carbon fiber elongated nose towards the tip of the vaginal shaped headlights, my index finger caressing the line down the middle of the light, as I release my other fingers and allow my palm to cup the round of her cheek. "Light dual-spring suspension, dramatic titanium exhaust system, and as they say in the write-up, 'Longtail DNA woven into every piece of this light supercar weighing in at 80kg less than other models.' You can't go wrong with the *McLaren*."

"So, why are you selling it?"

"I don't want my kid to have it when I die."

"Funny, that's why I want it," and I tell this stranger, this rich muther of a stranger, my tale. He really didn't care for it. Our paths crossing is more proof to him that he must get rid of this beast of speed. This sexy, daring, good as new at 2 years of age. Poor girl's been hooked up to life-support in this expansive garage filled with immaculate fast cars and glamourous vehicles. Why this one? Why does he care that his son doesn't inherit this one?

It is a cash deal. Bank transfer/wire to be more specific. I must leave my mail-order bride on life-support in this garage for a few more hours. Go to the bank. File the transfer, send the email confirmation, and then I will be back, my dear. Her door dimples are so smooth. Pat her tooshie and I'm back in my Mini Cooper putting it down the Hollywood Hills to a good old Bank of L.A.

$

He has removed her from the electric cords pumping life into a car coma. He had taken her for a short spin through the hills before I returned. She was outside, alone, in the curved driveway of this man's Southern California castle. I am dropped off by a car service. "You live here?" – "No, I bought that car." – "Damn." I get out, but before I can take a step or two the driver has leaned out the passenger window for my attention, "Hey, could you give me a couple good stars? A 5 star goes along way for us drivers." – "Yeah, sure." But I won't. Not because he doesn't deserve it or because I'm a dick, no; I'm in love and love is blind, deaf, and dumb.

Look at her in the sun. The fire light of Los Angeles. The city of angels, the city where dreams really do come true. Her transparent breast of a dome, bra size B, that reaches back to her tail, a raised ass, her license plate sticking out, letting everyone know who her daddy is. I'd fuck her pipe if I was a lover of shape and beauty, however darling, I prefer to sit back, naked, warmed by the heat collected from the sun on your leather seats. Sit back, tied in, bound to you, teasing you first with a little voom, vroom, then warming you up, slowly at first, let your oils swill and soak your barrings, vibrating under the hood, wanting more, begging me for more, and more I will give you, on the freeway, the free roads of this glorious country, however, if only we were in the UAE (United Arab Emirates), 160 km/h, our 99 mph, still too slow, but enough wiggle room to give her what she's made of.

The original owner taps on the window. Snaps me out of my, what once was a childhood delusion, now realistic zone. I step out. "Sorry, I was…" – "You're happy, I don't blame you." – "Transfer's been initiated," I tell him, reach out my hand to shake. He shakes, with the key-pod.

The pod is in my hand, my palm, for this car, this speed-queen, the daredevil of the Hollywood Hills. "I'll take great care of her," I assure him. Is it a loss for this man? I cannot tell. His eyes have no real expression. Distant, yet fully present. Was his story real? Maybe he doesn't even have a son. Might not even be married. Just a car collector. So then why set this one free? Why the fastest? Obviously custom designed, to a point, right? They always say custom, but it's not much different than choosing your preferred sauce for your chicken nuggets. Maybe he wanted a different interior than offered? He had to compromise. Compromise does not come easy to men of such stature. Me, however, I'm not one to choose, I'm just finally happy my dad's dead, and not because he's dead, but because Candy just started up with a tap of her button, from my finger, with her key-pod in my pocket. He taps the window with his knuckle again. Still in his driveway, thinks he can do whatever he wants. Zip down the window. Would have been cooler if you couldn't see the thin metal seem between the window and the pod-glass. Can't custom that away. "Yeah?" I ask. "Careful with the curves down the hill. Gets tight in some areas." – "I saw that. Any particular street to avoid?" – "All of them. Have fun." And now he walks away. I watch him. I want to see him enter his massive wooden doors. Disappear. Me alone with Candy. Humming. Hum, Candy, hum. "Let's go, dear," she says to me. My right hand obeys. My right foot obeys. As my thumb circles the dot button of her brake, the sole of my sneakers, good pair, lasted me five years now, presses against her foot brake. Hmmm—clop, I press her brake button. Really turns her on. Rev her, vroooooom, vroom, vroo000O000oommm.

There are a lot of buttons here. Tablet's not touch sensitive, seems archaic, but whatever. A bit spooked to toggle through the menus. Do I want the stereo? No. Just get out of here so you can get on the freeway.

You don't pay out three-hundred grand to stress and sweat this much trying to figure out how to change a gear on a car. This is the downside of buying used in the modern era of automation and too many options to scroll through, nearly impossible ways to customize menus, and probably have to register online, download an app, just to shift out of second gear. Rolling out of the driveway. I am rolling. I am moving my Candy. I am getting her out of this prison. Locked up for years, hooked up to life-support, neglected, unlaid, unrun, unwanted, and too seductive for all the rest. The gates open, I am rolling onto the muther fucking pavement. The well laid concrete of the driveway dips gently onto the pavement, however the next few feet looks like it had been de-mined by the LA national guard, and they did not bother to refill the holes. I've heard of that in Costa Rica. Don't pave the driveways, drive-roads to the homes. In fact, add some massive boulders and stones along the roadway so that no one bothers with a quick get-away, if not spending most of your time at home, feeding off the fruits of the jungle, so you do not replace your shocks every few months. The Hollywood Hills have no excuse. No one's pulling a fast get-away down these roads. 10mph is going to get you a head-on up here. And avoiding these potholes is really a disservice to our first ride together. No one likes rug burn on their first date, especially on their honeymoon.
"I'll buff your belly, baby," I promise Candy as we pass the last pothole, clear of a tire in a last hole, and able to roll up to about 6, seven mph around this long bend. This high up everyone has interior driveways, even letting their gardeners pull their *Toyota* pickups through the gates. Keep the overhauls off the skinny roads. That is going to change, and sooner than I expected. This bend leads me straight, well curving into an even thinner road. People have parked their *Prius'* half on the half-man walkway/sidewalk. The *Tesla's* been parked correctly, a real nuisance up here. I must roll her to a stop. The only way past this electric robbery is to get up on that sidewalk curb. Candy's gonna kill me. I swear

I'll get you all checked out once we get you home. A good bathing, buffering, a lot of love and attention. I lose my brace on the foot break. Candy rolls forward, auto-drive, more control than neutral. Her tire pushes against and up the curb. Her body is light; however she has her strength and we roll up along, back wheel up, front wheel back down, and our tail passes the *Musk* machine of death, allowing my foot to once again press upon my Candy's vroom, vroom. But not too much, there are plenty of half parked cars down this maze, and a crossroad will pop right out of the blue up here, whoa, break, slow brake; like this one, right here. "I like the way you braked for me," Candy hummmms.

$

The hills really could use a re-paving and widen these roads while they're at it. Use sky real estate, build up, not as close to the road as possible. You know over half these streets were done pre-regulation in the first place. You are all rich as fuck up here, redo these roads yourself. I just gave that guy my entire inheritance, that should fix those landmine relics outside his front door. Some of these houses are trashy at this point. Down there, on the other side, in the Valley, those flat one-story homes with a built-in driveway are refurbish-able, and cheaper than scraping the fifties home in a box. Up here you look like a washed up male pornstar hitting his late 70s, had gotten his law degree at a Riverside extension at 42 when everything went to internet, and he lost any sort of value. It wouldn't be until Two-Thousand Eight that he'd get a random call inviting him to be a Guest Autographer at a pornography convention in Anaheim. He had done a few movies with Ellen Days at the tail end of the Studio Camera era, and according to them, he can move a few hundred headshots from the day. His garage is filled with boxes of past videotapes, signed contracts 50-100 pages in length, magazines, duplicates of issues he's been spotlit in, in some way, even the few ads he posed for in *Diesel* Magazines during the NY Club Kid era. They had hired him for his pecks and abs. Everyone hired him for his pecks and abs -- Small dick, but that didn't matter, and the girls preferred it. A break from the gargantuan sloppers they are usually paid to "enjoy." None-the-less, some celebrity can scoop his house up and throw him in a down the hill home, tear the relic down and build up. Force widen the new road while they're at it. Make the widening trend. Everyone's gotta do it. "Have you passed Henry Elbuns' home?" they'll inquire with neighbors, "A delight. I didn't think twice about scrapping my side mirrors on anything."

$

Okay, stop sign, break. Take a moment. Look at this beauty. Make her talk. Talk to me, Candy. Whisper sweet nothings from your speakers. Scroll menu, menu two, scroll, menu, menu, scroll, *Sirius Radio*, no account, fuck it, Bluetooth. Classical music. Ride with pride, when you ride low and slow. Roll from the Stop Sign, cross the line, blinker, turn left, past a blue *Corvette* convertible waiting at its sign. A blonde. She doesn't take notice of me or Candy. That won't be the case once I cross back onto Sunset Blvd.

Car service took me some other way. This section has some breathing room. Probably takes longer. What do I care? Sunday drive, right Strawberry? – "I thought my name was Candy?" – "Strawberry's your pet name." – bump—stupid potholes. Ha, look at that, right there, someone with half-a-brain up here. Tore down his whole lot, extending the muther fucking street. Not loving the patch of gravel I must tread Strawberry over, but nobody said adventure was going to be easy.

GPS wants me to take a right. I'm taking another left for good measure. I've twisted around so much a left is basically a right now. Lumpy road. Tire light. Picked up a rock from the gravel. Lumpy ass road. Tire light. My Cooper's tire light's been on for years now. This is not a Cooper, this is a diamond greased in freedom. I pull to the side, as close as I can get to the sidewalk without halving the curb. Yeah, now I'm that asshole. It'll be just a minute. Raise the door. No one around to see me, to watch, to be impressed. Which tire has got the pebble? Front's look fine, passenger back, fine, oh fuck my god is that a fucking flat? A nail? I picked up a fucking nail!?!

"Are you fucking kidding me," I exclaim, "This is bullshit." Pull out my phone. No reception. No reception? What the fuck? Where am I, Iraq? No reception, really? I walk uphill, uphill will have reception. No reception. Nope. Still none. That's another ugly porn-hub. No reception. Fuck these hills are hardcore. They don't look it from a car, but walk this shit? This is crazy land. Okay, still nothing. Nothing. I'm looking out over the Hollywood Hills from a gap lot. Not sure if its recently emptied or been here for a minute. There is no for sale sign. No carpentry construction gear. Graveled out. About what you'd expect of overgrowth in So. Cal, but it's still hard to say if it's years or years. I gotta walk back to the car.

Downhill is much easier on the thighs. A nightmare for my ankles though. I didn't realize how weak my lower legs were. Thap, thap, goes the soles of my sneakers. They're low on traction, so I gotta make sure I slap the sole down and not slide it onto the pavement at this slope. Check reception, nope.

I lean up against Candy's ass. It's a bit boney from this angle. She's looking a bit haggard here squeezed against the curb. Did I scratch up the other tires? I don't dare look. What am I going to do about this, shit?

If I walk downhill, the roadside could drive me up with a spare? Yeah, what are they gonna do, leave me down there? No. That's the plan. Okay, Candy, you wait here. Arm yourself, don't want a coyote taking you for a joyride without me. I slap her ass and –Thap—Thap—I go down the Hollywood Hills and sundown's coming quick this time of year. Just changed the clocks. I'll miss the sunset. Probably just get to the bottom by then, if.

$

Seven o'clock. I took two wrong turns in there, but I'm breaking out to Franklin Blvd, and I got two bars on my fucking phone finally. I could have checked a few streets up, but I figured, get to a main road, somewhere that GPS will pick up and stick around at least. At least without a hic-cup. Eleven o'clock. I was starving. Hoofed it to a fast-food joint. I had a couple bucks to spend. That's it though. No more money for me. Just a wait for roadside.

One AM the next day. Always weird how we call night, night, generally, but when the news or someone serious points out the time past 11:59, they refer to it as the morning. When does 12:30 feel like morning? No shit, there's the tow. I really don't need the tow, a service with a spare will do. And that's what I tell him as I get into the passenger seat of truck. "No spare service, just a tow." He turns on his blinker and looks to cross traffic, "You got a place you like to take it?" – "I don't." – "Better search your phone buddy."

And I better do that fast before there is no service, phone service.

"Yeah, hi. Got a question for ya. You service tires for a *McLaren*?" I ask the only open 24hour service station in the area, Glendale. "He hung up on me," I tell the driver. "Did you say a *McLaren*? Like in the super-car?"

"Yeah," I tell him. When your new *McLaren* has a flat you do not feel flattered with impressing the tow truck driver.

"For real?"

"Yeah, for real. Stupid, picked up a nail way up there."

"You live up here?"

"Hell no, I live in West Covina. I just bought it from a guy here in the hills. Today, bought it today. Yesterday if you want to be precise about it."

"You can't take that kind of car to a lot at 1am, man," it's gotten really dark going up these windy roads, "You really can't take it to anywhere except their dealership, or whatever they might have. Either way, you're ordering a tire, not putting a spare on it. That's it, right?" We've illuminated Candy, in the dark, lonely, stalled, flat, gloomy. "Yeah, that's her."

"Sucks, dude," he stops, "Your best bet is to tow it to your house in West Covina. Let me turn this around somewhere up there and we'll get her hitched. Hop out."

I do just that. This sucks so hard.

-$

The reverse alarm –EEP! EEP!!—EEP!! EEP!!— Echoes and resonates through all the hills. Everyone on the street has woken up. Lights turn on there, lights over there, lights way down there. Lights across the dip in the hill. Whatever, at least it's a *McLaren* getting towed, not some *Tesla* with auto-kill. Love to race a *Tesla*. Get this tire fixed and smoke one of those rich assholes who gotta charge their car instead of pumping some good old gas and going for the gold. –EEP!! EEP—goes the tow bed, down, down, down—CACHANG! He stops it just before the pavement—Clunk, lunk, sounds—scrape—he scrapes the metal tow towards the front tires of my darling Strawberry. Sparks along the pavement, the asphalt. Sparks in the dark of the Hollywood Hills that is nearly illuminated by the vast electric grid that is LA and everything below.

-$

The driver's good. Gentle with the windy turns. Probably spooked to scratch my car. Should be. Don't fuck up, dude. I'm counting on you to know how to navigate— the truck justles forward and back. He's had to hit the brakes. Asshole from somewhere took that turn too fast and ignored our headlights. "This place is a bitch for entitled drivers," he tells me. "Yeah, I don't drive like that," I assure him. He doesn't believe me. Why should he. Look at me. Probably thinks I stole the car. Not his problem. The insurance checked out with dispatch, he's good to go. Not his problem, but he's pretty sure I swiped these keys. Thinking my brother's car? Maybe my wife's car. Left me. Fucking a Studio Exec. Invited me over to rub it in my face. Make me drive all the way up into the hills. Probably thinks I swiped the keys then. Left my Mini Cooper parked diagonally in his driveway, their driveway. This guy doesn't know me. Doesn't know how much this Fast Car means to me. Never in his life would he assume I considered this purchase my Father's last dying wish. That, I have nothing, nothing of value. Nothing but temp jobs. Temp cook at this diner, temp cook at that. Temp this food, temp over at that one. Thinks my dick's made of gold, not a limp lonely nothing of a cock to write home about and can barely spend more than sixty at a strip club per month. He wouldn't believe it even if he saw it. Nope not me. I'm just another entitled asshole, who for whatever reason, lives out in the burbs of the burbs, just a couple blocks from the 10 freeway. He won't believe it when we drop the car off. He'll be sure to call the cops to find a ransom for the car. He's got the plates. I'll be dealing with that in an hour or so. "Yeah, take a right under the freeway," I tell him, JOLT—He hits the brakes again. A rent-a-car speeds by us, passes us under the overpass. Fn' psycho. I can see it's a rental from the plate frame. "I'm just around the next block. Follow that asshole," I tell my driver as the headlights of the rental disappears down the block.

--CRASH—not us, but we hear it. It's pretty massive of a hit, we can tell. "Right," I tell him. We turn the corner. Fire down the block. The hit was on my block. Fucked up. We keep rolling down the block. "You on the other side of that?" he asks me. "Yeah. Fuck, go around the block before the firetrucks block us off." –EEP! EEP!—I can't watch. This guy has to reverse a few houses before we can get out of here –EEP! EEP!—Two more houses—EEP! EEP!— he stops before rolling my *McLaren* across the intersection—EEP! EEP!—"You want me to get out? Gide you?" I ask. My hand already on the door handle. "No, I got it." –EEP! EEP!—He rolls it back. Back. Slow. Back. Back. And the back of the truck crosses the corner and it looks good. We're okay. "Okay, great, go that way," I point down the street where he will be able to circle around to the other side of the blazing fire. "No sirens yet. I think we're okay," I assure him, reassure myself. We turn the corner of my block. That fire is brighter on this side. Now we hear a siren in the distance. "We have to do this fast," the driver tells me as we continue rolling closer towards the fire. "Which one is yours?"—Oh, my god—"That one," and I am pointing, in shock, in horror, stunned, at a loss, pointing at my home. My one bedroom, one car garage, one bath, kitchenette of a home. The home that has a burning rental car attached to the cement porch.

I watch my house being cooked, but it is tin. The flames flap against the tin-siding. The roof of my home has caught a blaze. And the tow drops the McLaren with a flat in my driveway, but partially on the sidewalk as to not get burned. And when the fire department and police show up, they instruct me that once they clear the scene, I best get another tow to move my car off the sidewalk before they call a tow to do it. The fire's out. Everything is soaked. The roof had to be soaked, that leaked into the living area. It's a disaster. I have this terrible underbelly of a feeling my homeowners will not be covering this. I'll have to file a case against the rental company. Not my fault he was drunk, speeding, and now dead. I was in my tow. He passed us. I knew it wasn't a good sign. Who passes someone under an overpass? And Candy's gotta get a push up the drive and off the sidewalk. I ask a firefighter as he rolls in the hose. "You think your guys could lend me a hand pushing my car up the drive?"

"Yeah, we're not allowed to do that. Against protocol."

The neighbor across the street has come out to watch the commotion. Others already went back in. I could ask him. I don't know him. He's a bit heftier than I. Maybe? "I'll take you on a drive?" It's a deal. He nods, "Yeah, for a ride."

-$

I'm exhausted. I've been taking the bus for a couple years now. Drops me off on the other side of the overpass. The walk is always an awkward reminder of how long it takes to get the claims debated, investigated, appealed, repealed, denied, corrected, approved, delayed. But nothing hurts like the reminder in the driveway. The reminder that the last of my small family had passed. That I was alone. My uncles had no children, and I had no siblings. It was always only me. I inherited the whole lot. It wasn't much, but they had collected what they could to leave me a little to make things a little better for this short order cook with five-year-old sneakers. And I have come home from my more stable cook gig at a diner in downtown LA. It's a two-hour bus ride there and back. Always a bit burnt by the end of the walk. I stop. Look at the tarp on my roof blowing in the wind. The wind from the freeway just over there. The speeding sounds of machines that travel to and from everywhere and anywhere. And in there. In my garage, my fast car, on life-support, still without a tire.

NO HARM, NO FOWL

My Dad's the coolest dad. Bet you want to know what makes my dad so awesome? He's rich. Like super rich. But that's not it. My dad's super powerful. He says, tells me all about it at supper. Dad never misses supper. Maybe a few due to work, but most of the time Dad, Mom, and me eat dinner everyday together as a perfect family. Mom cooks, and she's a good cook, Dad says. She makes really good pudding, that's what I think. Oh, my dad. He tells me how he has hundreds of men who work for him. And what they do is so cool. They pump oil out of the ground. I'm totally serious. Like you know the stuff you put in your car? Not our car, our car's special, runs on electricity and water. Dad says it lasts longer and drives farther. Cool, huh? Get this, he's got a private jet that does the same thing. When I grow up I want to be like Dad.

My uncle's coming to visit this weekend. He's a libarial. Cool, but not as cool as Dad. What is kinda super cool about Uncle Hey is that he lives on a farm. Like a huge farm. He's like a real cowboy. Always brings us the best hamburger meat when he visits. Dad eats the steak he brings, but I eat the hammmburrrgeeerrrs, with balsamic vinargets, and toasted buns. Mom cuts the onions. Uncle Hey doesn't have a married person. He says he likes being single. Cool, but not as cool as having a mom.

Did you know Dobermann's brains grow bigger than their skulls? I want to be like a Dobermann. Then I'd be super smart. I told Dad that I was going to invent a new water that uses the oil he pumps and turns it into even better oil. He told me I was a genius. I know. I'm really smart. I get straight As and I don't even have to go to school with the other kids. I get to go to home school. I got a teacher who lets me learn whatever I want. She's cool too. She's a native American. They were here before us. They made the land oil by killing all the dinosaurs. I told her she should become a doctor and make new dinosaurs for my dad so we never run out of oil. She said I had a wild imagination. That's because I'm smart!

I turn eight next week. That's why Uncle Hey's coming to visit. We are going to have a big party with rides and stuff. I have a lot of friends that always come to my parties. Because I don't go to school, or play sports or stuff, I only see my friends at our parties. I think I'm getting a super gigantic black lava dark chocolate cake with silver icing. That's what I told Mom I needed, so I'm sure I'll get it. I usually get what I want, if I really want it. That's not true. I always get what I want. Dad doesn't though. Lately Dad has been complaining that we are not getting enough water, rain water in California. He complains about it all the time. Says it is ruining his investment in Uncle Hey's farm. Stupid right? Why is the rain mean to my Dad? I think it's stupid and should rain more. Rain should always fall from the sky for my Dad.

.:.:.

Uncle Hey's here. I can hear his car pulling up. He'll find me out here on the back deck. Sunny today. Sunny everyday. Way too sunny. Not a cloud in sight. "Hey there little fella, whatcha doin' out here bare naked in the scalding sun?" asked Uncle Hey. "I'm rain dancing," I tell him, spin around, tap my left foot three times, tap my right foot five times, fart, hop twice, and shake my hands into the sky. "You're not a Native American, little guy. Shouldn't be doing stuff that ain't yours to do," he scolds me. I figured he'd have some libarian attitude. Dad warned me. Said not to let Uncle Hey catch me praying for rain. Said he wouldn't think it was proper. "I'm praying for rain, Uncle Hey," I tell him, totally defying my father and annoying Uncle Hey.

.:.:.

Dad's wheeled the charcoal up from the shelter. I can see him scoop a scoop at a time as I spin, stop, scoop, spin, stop, scoop, spin, stop, scoop and into the black iron BBQ. Uncle Hey sets the fire as I do my hovering cloud squats— UP—squat n' hover the land—UP—squat n' hover the land—UP! "Why don't you pee while your wee-wee's down there little man," Uncle Hey joshes me. Pay no mind. No harm, no foul. The rain is all that's hallow, the rain must come before tomorrow! Shake-ka-Skake-ka-Shake-Ka!

The stars map out more constellations than usual. The sky so clear, even Neptune has a thumbprint, and our neighboring galaxies have their TVs on; sports, their team is winning, it's the last game of the season. Father hands me a Hamburger as I bird pose upon my single left big toe. "Ketchup?" I ask. He removes the bun for me. Gives the burger a little ketchup squirt and twists the bun right back on. "Thanks, Daddio," I say, take a bite, and let my chew become the dance that must call the rain so my Father may pump the oil so we may reign supreme and be happy and cool. May the rain follow the rhythm of the chewing of the meat. Chew-burger. Chew-Chew-Cow-Cow-Chew. Chew-Burger-Chew-Chew-Chew-Chew.

.:.:.

.:.:.

.:.:.

.:.:.

.:.:.

.:.:.

.:.:.

.:.:.

.:.:.

.:.:.

.:.:.

.:.:.

.:.:.

.:.:.

.:.:.

.:.:.

.:.:.

.:.:.

The house alarm is sounding. Everybody's phone alert systems are sounding. Dad runs past my bedroom. I gotta go after him. Something serious is happening. In the sitting room, the TV alert system is sounding. Dad looks at me. The remote-control shakes in his hand. "What did you do?" he questions me. Stern. Cruel. Accusing. "I didn't do anything?"

"He prayed for rain," Uncle Hey says from across the room. "That's ridiculous," waves off my Mother, fixing herself a drink. It's dark still. 3:30am. "I don't see any rain," I complain with my face pressed against the window. Father pulls me away from the glass. "Stay away from the windows," he warns me. "We should make a plan," he looks to Uncle Hey. "Your Helicopter?"

"Out of service."

"We drive now, take a plane from inland."

"We're getting the alerts because of the roads."

"Boat?"

"Boat."

.:.:.

.:.:.

.:.:.

.:.:.

.:.:.

.:.:.

.:.:.

On the docks we can get a better view of the surrounding cloud layers. The sun is just beginning to illuminate even from its hiding. The clouds are being illuminated. They are dark. Serious. Harrowing. I am proud. We are awaiting our

ride. The ship is not here. Father had made the call. It is coming from another port. The wind is picking up. Mother has gotten sand in her eye. The water level seems to have lowered. The calm before the storm. "How long have you had a drought out here?" Uncle Hey yells over the whistling winds. "Eight, nine years!" Dad replies. "That makes for a lot of dry land out there!" Hey yells. "It'll all flood for sure," Dad's confident, but not happy. "Dad?" I ask, "If it floods, does that wash all the oil away?"
"No, that's a stupid thing to think."
"Good," I say, worried I had messed up the only hope we had to save our family, the world.

.:.:.

.:.:.

.:.:.

.:.:.

I can see the boat in the distance. "There it is," I tell them, but the sandstorm is getting too hard to look out over the ocean anymore. I'm little, I can do it easier than them. Mom can't even keep her face uncovered. Dad has his back to the wind, and Uncle Hey's smart and wearing his sunglasses with his shirt wrapped around his face. The tide has gotten even lower. I guess not lower, but farther away. Tugging on Hey's pant leg, "I say we make a run for it." He's considering it. How far until we hit water again? Will we be close enough to the boat to swim out? Mom is not going to run. I don't think Mom has ever run in her life. Dad, he'll have another heart attack if he runs. But if I run, and Hey runs with me, we can get to the boat, maybe take the boat to get an off-roader and get back here to save Mom and Dad. "Did you say, 'Off-Roader?'" Dad asks me, his hands covering his eyes, his lips spitting sand from his tongue. "Yeah!" – "We have one! We have one in the gardener's shed!" Dad has put his arm around Mom. He's yelling into her ear about going back to the house. She takes the first step, eager to get off the dock. It's a hard walk back. The wind is ferocious, and the sand has begun to hit us so hard our skin is becoming irritated. The stairs, wooden windy stairs up the Northern California cliffside are slippery when wet, more slippery when covered in a sheet of slick dry sand. Mom has nearly slipped to her death a number of times now. Uncle Hey has taken it upon himself to assist her the rest of the way up as Dad slowly takes his walk one step at a time with a firm grip on the handrail. I'm at the top eager to get to the off-roader and go zoom-zoom over all these awesome new sand dunes forming everywhere.

From way up here you can kinda tell that the sand isn't being blown around from the beach. Nah, the sand is like totally raining down from the clouds. It's raining sand from sand clouds. Crazy cool. And you know what I think. That's right. Oil comes from the desert and rain is the devil of the desert, so my prayer was wrong but actually totally right! I gotta do another dance. Get this storm really going. Clear all the sand from the deserts to the oil is even easier to reach! Make my Daddy rich forever. So, I start dancing again as my family slowly makes their way up the cliffside.

.:.:.

.:.:. dance to the rhythm dance to the thunders dance to boulders that tumble down the mountains dance with the stubble and the trouble and the rubble dance to the…Hey grabs me by the arm. "Stop that! Stop all of this. You are making a mockery of sacred beliefs."

.:.:.

.:.:. Dad's finally reached the last step. Hey helps him toward us. "Where's the shed?" Hey asks him. "Down the valley behind the house. Beside the creek." .:.:. But that is all filled with sand by now. "I'm going inside," Mother says turns toward the house. "Which way?" she asks. "This way," and Dad leads her back towards the second floor of the house, trudging through the sand. Hey grabs me, drags me along with him to the house. He kicks in the glass window. Sand pours into the second-floor bathroom. Hey helps Father in, who helps Mother in, and then I hop in, and Hey follows.

.:.:.

I am so jazzed up about all this. Hyper as can be. Hey made us all get out of the bathroom so he could close the door, stop the sand from coming in. I already ran downstairs to one of the guestrooms to see how fast the sand would come in way down there. It came in fast. Super fast. I'm back upstairs now. I couldn't get the door closed. Not strong enough. No one gonna notice. Everyone's too worried about everything else. "Dad, what are we going to do?" I ask when I find him sitting on the edge of his bed, alone. He doesn't respond. "Where's Mom?" He doesn't respond. Oh, well. I turn around. Mom's dead on her master bathroom floor. Gunshot to the head. Suicide. That's when you murder yourself. My grandfather suicided himself too. "Is Mom dead?" No answer. I go out to find Uncle Hey. He's not in the hall. He's not in his guestroom. He's on the roof. Duh. That's totally smart. I gotta get up on the roof.

.:.:.

There is no getting on the roof. The sand has poured in from the hole up there. Maybe if I dig. I gonna dig. Dig. dig dig dig dig dig dig dig dig dig. Phew – "HEY! HEY!" I yell at him, yards away from me. The winds have died down; however the pouring sand rain has not let up. I trudge my way toward my uncle as the grains rise higher and higher up his legs, past his knees by the time I'm there. "Don't stop dancing, boy," he tells me, contradicting himself from earlier. I scootch around. The sand has reached the middle of my uncle's thighs. Soon it will pass his waist. Scootch I do. Move and I won't get buried. "Dance with me, Uncle Hey," I advise, "That way you won't drown."

"I'm too old to dance, son. Like your father was too old

to dance with your mother, I am too old to dance; for there is no humidity for my sweat to fowl." He was mad by the time the sand covered his head. Mad with confusion. Mad with grief. Mad at the world. Mad at me. I scootched. Scootched and scootched. Not sure what to do next, but I know if I keep on scootchin' then someone'll come and scratch this itch. . . .:.:.

FAHRENHEIT TWO TWENTY

"You like that?" I say, just under my breath, "You do. Just like that . a little more . deeper . Oh, you really like it. Mmm, here let me join you." I don't have to get ready, I've been ready. Ready for twenty minutes now to find a truly hot girl on this site. Some days are better than others. Some searches are quick and to the point, she's sexy, she's young, she's hot, and hot for it. Others tease you with a thumbnail. Just a little bit to get you thinking you're visually mated through pixels. Click the thumbnail and disappointment fills the air after the short ten second commercial. She's cute, I guess, but not Hot. Hot is hot. There is no comparison. An attractive girl can be hot, sure, but attractive does not equal hot. Hot is the top rungs of a ladder. You had to step over the others to reach the Sun.

LIcKarus!

He is me, for women. I am LIcKarus, the lover of all Hot Women, hot girls, hot ladies, but unlike the foolish Icarus, I do not seek glory, nor admiration for my conquests, no; I seek to only lickafile hot girls. I am just that basic. Really, is that too much to ask for? May all the other women be fully satisfied by the men of the world, if only God would see to it, I only have to fuck the hot girls till the day I die. Amen. "Oooughh," I jerk forward, catch myself before I soil my drawers wrapped around my ankles.

^

BEEP – BEEP – BEEP – My pager. I'm needed at the hospital. Another day, another need of me. I swish my jacket on, swing my keyring along my index finger, pocket them, don't bother with a wallet, keep all my info on my phone, and all an ER surgeon needs is his phone, his pager, and his keys. My driver's license sits in the *Porsche's* glove compartment with the registration.

I always open the garage from the kitchen, start the car from the hallway, and alarm the house as I pull out onto the drive. The drive's a good fifty yards from the gate to the road. Gives good runway for me. Camera's outside the gate warn me of oncoming traffic so I give 'em time to pass before I speed out at 65 to get to the hospital in time. Save a life. Save a life or two. Get to that gurney on a wing and a prayer. Va-rooooooommmm…….*Gold Digger* is my favorite song. Now you see why I pray to the lord above. It is merely to assure my status compares to the ideal that I only fuck the hot girls? I think you do. Come on. Spend a day with me. Florida. Home of the accidental needs of the needy. This way, Miami hospital central. Varoooooom.

^

Multiple gunshot wounds, multiple victims, I have to make a decision. I'm good with decisions. I scrub in. I have them prep both. The choice is easy. One is a boy of thirteen years of age, bullet wounds to the abdomen, bullet wounds to the thigh, the other a boy of ten years of age bullet wounds to the legs and feet. We will treat the thirteen-year-old, keep him alive, save the other's mobility if we have time.

^

I scrub out. The ten-year-old will walk with a limp. By the time he's in college he can get that fixed up cosmetically if he gets a good job. I dry my hands. Step out of the washroom, down the hall to the waiting room. The boys' families rise in unison. Someone's older sister is gorgeous. We are talking a nine point six out of ten. She's bordering perfection and what's unreal about it all is meeting her at her most vulnerable boosts her potential to a ravenous nine point eight and I'm going to play this as well as I can no matter who's brother she belongs to. "They are both in wonderful condition," I tell the room. They all break down in tears. I look her right in the eye. She catches the look. It is quick. If I had dawdled, given too much attention to the mother or a father first, another brother would have gotten the first tear of joy and appreciation, however, with the speed of a hawk, it is my pupil that catches her first tear of joy, and she smiles, at me, her savoir.
^

I make her cum, backwards, in a changing room as the families visit the boys. She is faint. Dizzy in fact as I pull out. "Sit," I tell her, assisting her down onto a cold, plastic chair. I've instinctually touched her forehead, "You're burning up," I recognize the unusual nature of the moment. "I'll be okay," she says, nearly falling out of the chair. I help her up and kneel beside her. We are both naked, but nothing is unusual other than this woman is suddenly seriously ill. Her color is off. She is very warm to the touch. I grab a thermometer from the corner, take her temperature. 108 degrees Fahrenheit. "My god," I find her a robe, throw it around her, quickly throw my clothes on. I have to get her back to the ER. Just down the hall. How do I explain this? My god, she's naked, but she's going to die… "Come on,"

I say, as I pick her up, draping her arm over my neck, drag her, carry her out the door, down the hall, find the first gurney and drop her on it. One, two, three, go!

^^^

Coast is clear. Why do they make these doors so heavy? Doesn't help in transporting objects. I've got her propped against the doorframe as my foot holds the monster door pried opened. I'm going to let the door ease her into the hall as I refoot myself so I can drag her better. She is conscious, yet has dropped like a dead weight. "Come on. I need you to pull yourself up a little," I tell her. "I am," she mumbles. Something is seriously wrong with her. The door to the ER from here is about 25 yards or so. Doesn't seem so far until you're walking it with dead weight. Dead weight radiating heat only comparable to a human oven.

^^^

A few yards from the double doors and her skin has begun to burn. The moisture in the air around her has turned to steam and the heat is only getting hotter in here for the both of us. "We're almost there," I assure you. "Will I ever see you again?" she asks, well knowing the answer would most likely be no for a myriad of reasons, either death, professionalism, life in general, separate ways, jealousy, or chaos; none-the-less, she asked as we reached the doors. Her eyes glazed and glassy. Her skin crisp and boiled. Her fever, deadly. "Get some rest," and remind her, "We saved your brother." The doors open, they place her on a gurney, "You saved my brother," and they wheel her away. I'm not sure what's occurred. Best not to pry. Best to leave it be. Shit, her clothes.

^^^

I have taken her belongings and given them to a loyal nurse. You know the kind. The ones that don't give a shit what you do as long as you don't do it to them or their daughters. Yeah, that nurse, Carol. Carol's cool. Carol's been here forever. Carol's made sure the worst of the best keep people alive as their mishaps stay in the bay. Why? Because we're the best and we do actually want to keep people alive, despite everything else we like to do while being alive. Carol also gets the cleanest coke, molly, and heroin. No fentanyl nothing. Tests it all here before she moves it too. Why tell you? Because we'll all be dead before the story's done. That's my guess. No more for me to do today so I go home and knock another one out before hitting the hay.

∧

BEEP-BEEP-BEEP
Va-Roooom- Suicide Attempt. Multiple stab wounds. Multiple victims. Two women. Gonna scrub in. My hands are soft. My fingernails always clean, always trimmed and filed. My cuticles always soft. The latex gloves always snap tight like a complete thin layer of blue skin. I will save them both.

∧

After the surgeries I am curious about my previous conquest. I've cleaned myself up, however I'll wear my top surgeon shirt and lapel to roam the ER.

I go from curtain to curtain. Door to door. She may have been moved already. Twelve hours? Probably gone after six. Maybe I'll? "Excuse me," I stop a nurse, "A young woman, with an extremely high fever was admitted last night?"

"B-102," she tells me, continues down the hall, disappearing behind a curtain. B-102? I'm at A-003. I turn and head east. She's still here. It wasn't a hot flash. It is something serious. Maybe I should turn around, just leave, and not visit her. Do not turn this corner, shit I turned the corner. I'm being drawn to her room. The Bs are rooms. No curtains. These ER rooms are rooms, rooms with ventilators and the likes. She's probably unconscious. I should look. Terrible things the human body can do to us. B-100, B-102. I look through the rectangular window. Through the wired mesh hashtagged through the glass. It is dark with only a single florescent light on beside the bed and the illumination of mechanical LEDs. I open the door. I enter. I can feel the warmth of the room as the door cracks open. A rush of heat exits as if trapped inside the vacuum of this space. I enter. Within an instant I begin to sweat.

^

The door closes behind me. The clasping sound of the metal door handle clamping closed. The glass behind me has fogged from my immediate perspiration. There are no ventilators. There are however a number of humidifiers doing their best to combat the heat resonating from her naked body on the bed in the middle of the small room. She has multiple IVs. Her body is so hot she is in need of extreme fluids. She can turn her head. She is weak, but she can see me. She can smile. She can spread her legs. She can still want me. I step back, back up against the wall. I am aroused. Disturbed by myself. Her pelvis presses into the air asking for me. I want her. My body wants her. The heat from her. My body knows she is wet. I can see her dripping onto the mattress. I have never been so aroused. Even when I first had her, no matter how, no matter when, it did not compare to now. I lock the padlock, switch off the single florescent and proceed to fuck this steaming hot woman, young twenty something woman, for a second time, and cum in her belly button.

∧

I've left her with nothing more to say. She was exhausted. I was uneasy. Pulled up my pants, unlocked the door, turned her single light back on, unlocked the door, left, and clocked out for the night. For the week. They have a number of other Doctors they have on-call. I need the week away from this woman. I'm going to get myself in trouble. There are plenty of hot girls in the sea. One's that are not dying.

∧

I've dined at Mick's Steakhouse along Dock 8. A few power plastic surgeons and bone marrow experts. We've all decided to play cards bi-monthly, however this week Allen's got a function upstate with his wife, so we all did surf n' turf before I found my way to Kells. Kells is my favorite strip-club south of Miami. I come to Kells every four months. When the girls rotate out for the season. I don't bother with the same strippers. Never bother with the same strippers. Things are cold tonight. Lots of lookers. More than usual. I can count the sevens and eights with two hands, that's unusual. Never that many lookers out here. This is off season? I check my watch. "Nice smart watch," a girl says as her fingernails grace my neck. She's a four. Go away. I ignore her. 11:49pm. I should have hit a bar for a little while. I'm too early for the hot ones. "Let's welcome to the stage Cinder, Tinder, and Kindling, the triplets that dance together, strip together, and do just about whatever together." Of course I am going to look up from my watch. That introduction needs no introduction. And the universe slows down. The drapes that had been still along the edge of the stage have moved. The spotlights have zipped into position freezing upon the corner, the mist, mystery, the fog, oozing from behind the drapes as three of the hottest women, early, early twenties, Hindi decent, with bindis, full breasts, full hips, thin waists, beautiful, sultry, slowly, in the slow motion of the greatest of movies take their positions on their independent poles as the music begins.

I may not have noticed how busy the club was if not for the three men who rudely have stepped in front of my table blocking my view. I can't see past these three. Sit the fuck down. They can't because there is nowhere to sit around the stage. Those seats are full. Men are throwing money at the triplets. I would like to throw some money. If I don't then they won't make their rounds toward me after their dance. Out of the corner of my eye I can see one of the triplets sandwiching a man's face with her breasts. They're that open. That hot? That open? "Excuse me?" I tap one of the guys blocking me. He does not respond. Come on. "Excuse me?!" I ask, louder, tap him again. He turns around. I wave him to the side. He points to himself. Who the fuck else would I be talking to? "Yeah, I can't see," I tell him. He has a burley face. Dock worker face. Turns his back on me. Muther fucker. The song ends. Guys are chitter chattering amongst themselves until the next song starts right up and the girls start dancing again. The club has raised a few degrees since they got on stage and I'm not going to miss this second song. I get up and push my way to the front. No seat but I'm gonna stand and throw some money. Let these three know, I'm the big fish to catch tonight. Not these blue-collar losers. Me. I'm the Miami surgeon you're gonna fuck in the back of the club thinking you caught the big fish. And I shower them with a stack of twenties, and yes, one of the three sees it and her pussy drips right there on stage and she ignores me just like a good little tease and finds me after they freshen up after their dance.

∧

"You really a doctor?"
"Yeah. An ER Surgeon."
"Dang, you make that much money?"
"Plastic Surgeons and ER Surgeons. We make the same.

Difference is I actually save lives."

"That's pretty hot."

"Do you own a boat?"

"Two."

Sister in pink takes my ring finger.

"You're not married."

"Never."

"You're a liar," she tells me.

"Not so. I'm as single as they come," I assure her.

"Maybe you're gay?" the one in purple says as she presses her cheeks against my erection, "Oh, maybe not."

"Why don't you marry us?" asks the yellow one.

"All three of you?" I ask.

"It's only fair," she says.

"What if you're bad in bed?"

"Do we look like we're bad in bed?" she says rubbing her breasts against my chest and up against my cheek. I let her nipple fall into my lips and out again.

"I'm too rich to take chances," I say, and that's when I notice how hot they all really are. Not physically. Well physically, but temperature, not visually. They are hot visually. Like the hottest girls ever. Hotter than the woman from the ER. But that's not it. Oh my god, they all just took their bottoms off. They're not supposed to do that. They want me. They've pulled me out. One is already on top of me. Oh, we're fucking. So fast, this is all happening so fast. If security comes back here…I can't speak, a sister is kissing me, the other eating at my neck, I see the drape of the VIP area opening, the bouncer entering, walking, stomping directly toward us. I cannot get up. Three women are too much for me. He's getting closer. I finish, can't help it. He pulls her off me, pelts me in the face, I'm immediately knocked unconscious.

^

I've come to in the back of a sedan. At least I think it's a sedan. Second thought I feel higher up, could be an Escalade, Suburban? I'm laid out in the back. Someone's driving. Where are we going? My face hurts. Wet with blood. He broke my nose. Driver's switched on his turn signal. Click, Click, Click. Making a left. My wrists are zip tied. Ankles too. All for extras? They set me up. Turn signal, another left.

^

We drove around for what seemed a good thirty minutes or so. Maybe we took a short stint on a highway, but most of it was stop and go stoplights and residential streets. We're finally at our destination. We're pulling into a garage. The door's closing behind us. "I'm supposed to leave you here," the driver says, gets out, closes the door behind himself. I listen to him leave. I can hear his steps. I can hear him open the door to the house. The squeak of the hinges, the closing of the latch behind him, and the overhead lights turn off. One – Breath. Two – Breath. Three, I sit up. I am in a dark garage. What do they want with me? Dumb question. They want my money. The door opens. Light comes in from the house. A person is entering, their body obscuring the illumination. They are darkness. A complete shadow of a person making their way towards my passenger window. The overhead lights turn on. It is one of the triplets. She is at the car door, opening it. "What do you want with me?" I yell at her. She stumbles back, weak, catching herself against a countertop. There is a moment. She helps herself back to stability. I see she has snips in her hand. "Give me your wrists," she says, weak. She sounds like a completely different person from an hour ago. I give her my wrists. She snips the ziptie. My hands are free. She squats, snips my ankle tie. My feet are free. She stands. She becomes dizzy. I give her my hand. "Are you okay?" I ask her. "No, something's wrong with us," she tells me. "Us, all three of you?"

"Yes, all three of us."
I've instinctually taken her hand. She's lost all pigment. Her skin is warm, hot to the touch. She is burning up, like in the club. Like the woman in the ER. "Where are your sisters?"

^

She takes me to them. They're in the shower. Cold shower. Sitting in the bath, in a pile of melting ice. I'm standing in the doorway of the bathroom. I don't know what to think. Yes, I do. I step over to the sink. I wash, gently wash the blood from my face. My nose is sore. Hurts. I am not happy about my nose. I take a hand towel, pat my face dry and then wrap a bundle of ice in it and press it on my face before addressing the "hotties" in the tub. "Did you get vaccinated?" I ask them. "From Covid?" one of them in the tub asks with the shivers. "Yeah," I say. "Yeah, we got it." I shrug, "You can still get it. What about the flu? You get your flu shots?"
"We're strippers, we get all our shots."
"What's stripping have to do with getting your shots?"
"Can you give us medicine?"
"Medicine?" I look at the sister beside me. She is propping herself up against the sink. What is wrong with these girls? "For what?"
"For whatever's wrong with us?"
"Someone probably drugged you."
"Nobody drugged us," one of them from the bath says, turns off the running shower.
"People drug girls like you all the time."
"Are you going to help us?" the one leaning on the sink asks, begs me, tugs on my shirt sleeve. "I don't know what you want me to do." The sisters are getting out of the tub. I feel inclined to assist them. If they slip and fall, I will feel responsible. This is strangely suddenly all of my fault. I am unclear why I feel this way, but I do. "Let's get you two to the bedroom," I say with their arms draped over my

shoulder. We leave the third anchored against the sink. Her knees are sure to buckle if she takes a step on her own at this point. She watches us leave down the hall. Her eyes tear. She is sad. Why? What is she saddened by? She whispers, under her breath, "I love you."

^

I rest them both on the bed. They are grateful. They both have beautiful, desirable eyes. Eyes that not only want to be desired, but eyes that seem to only desire me at this moment. "Lay with us," they say, in unison. The first time I have heard them speak in such a way. As a man, I have fantasized of such. Twins speaking in unison as they seduced me, but never, even with the money I have acquired, have I bothered to fulfil such a dream. Their sister is still in the bathroom. Do I get her? I look back, down the hall. Her sisters are pulling on me. They want me now. But aren't they ill? A ruse? But why? "Lay with us," they desire again, their fingers now against the skin of my wrists. Their fingertips hot, burning. Ow. Hurts. I pull my arm away. "What?" they ask. "Scratched me," I assume. "Come," they say. "Your sister," I want them to let me get their sister. They roll upon each other. Moan. "Come," they say. "But your sister," I say. "Hurry," they say, "We're burning up. We're..." and they begin to fornicate with each other. Sisters engaging in lustful sexual activity as I rush down the hall to retrieve their sister we had left alone in the bathroom.

^

"I want to see my sisters," she says immediately seeing me in the doorway.
"That's why I came back," I tell her. I take her hand. Her hand is hot to the touch. I can't touch it. Hurts. "What's the matter?" she asks. "You're too hot," I tell her.
"Why are you saying that? " she is bothered.

"I don't mean. I mean hot to the touch," and I demonstrate that when I touch her palm, I nearly burn myself.
"What's happening to me?" she asks, her eyes that of a child, a child stricken with an illness certain to kill her before her time. "I don't know. Let's get you to your sisters."

∧

Why bringing her to her lustful sisters would be salvation for the triplet in her most vulnerable is beyond me, however it was the right thing to do as they accepted her into their bed, as they are a family and together, they comforted each other, until it became clear that the comforting was not for them, no, the performance was completely designed for my unadulterated arousal. An arousal so great that I could not withstand the magnetic pull of them all as I disrobed and joined them on the mattress.
And for the next hour I indulged in sex play at scalding hot degrees only to find myself in the same ER that I have been steadily employed at for several years. Now on a specially designed gurney for third degree burns. Burns that cover my entire body. Even the soles of my feet have been blistered from the constant licking by the triplets. My penis unfortunately so severely burned it has become dried flesh and my friend; the same colleague I had eaten with the same evening had done the surgery to remove the useless extremity from my body.

NAME

Ever since I can remember, I desired a purpose. Something tangible. Something spiritual. Something cosmic and grand. A purpose that no other had had before me. A unique purpose. A purpose, that if we are lucky, would impact the world, possibly even the outer reaches of our atmosphere. When I say we, I mean, you and I, you being everything that is not myself. I have always prayed for a purpose, not to live a life with a lump on my log, or my branches too weak to lift a tire. No. I want a purpose so grand that even the floral would uproot to witness the purpose in action. A purpose. What a wonderful word. I am no linguist, so I know nothing of its originality, construction, or why a word such as purpose would even need a purpose beyond the one you and I might discover, or be granted in our short, but possibly useful lifetime.

It would be difficult to have counted the hours I have been alive, growing. There were many wonderful hours. Hours of clear skies. Hours of immaculate clouds. There were even rainy days that were so exquisite in its downfall, its pitter patter upon everything, that it was as if we were all in a dream together. I have never seen snow. I have been witness to a number of stories of great slopes, gondola rides, the difference between an intermediate slope and an advanced slope. A black diamond represents the Advanced slopes. Isn't that fascinating. Using the color of coal, yet in the shape of a diamond. I must admit, although it is embarrassing, and you may find me utterly naïve, I too have never seen the leaves change. I do not live in that environment and never will.

@

There was a squirrel that got in a fight with a bird over a twig the other day. Bird was sitting on the twig when a squirrel came by and attacked the bird. It didn't last long. The bird flew away. I saw no point in the interaction, and I told no one about it. That is why life is meaningful.

@

Can you guess what shape is upside down when the face is in a corner and the roots are perpendicular to a comet? Didn't think so. Neither can I. I wish I had a purpose.

@

Sometimes a boy comes around and climbs to the top of me. He pisses from the branches and shits in the clouds. I call him a blessing and he calls me a blemish on capitalism. We both don't know how to vote. He's underage. I'm stuck in the mud.

@

Knock knock.

Who's there?
Karma. So Tan.
Karma So Tan, Who?
Karma So Tan you wanna ocean?

@

Redwood nation will rise again, and when they do…

@

Take care fair bear, the snare is in the dare.

@

Said the hare to the mare,   air is like prayer
And prayer is like air

And the feathers that flock together are prayers of a feather forever and never and ever and lever yourself to the purpose, that I wish and I wish I and I wish I may.

@

A form of light reflects from the dew on my leaves,
Shine,
The coil of the copper snake that eases between the tablets,
Of you and the girl on the other side of my trunk.
Romance spins like yarn in the grass that grows, dries, and dies in the fields that spread from the dirt in which my roots grabble with.

A thirst.

Do the people around me have a thirst? Do their toes toggle upon the concrete in search of water, the meaning of life?

A hunger?

I have no hunger. That is a grave difference between me and them. They must chew their food to survive. Osmosis is how my kind bares the basics.

@

Another storm has split my upper trunk. A brisk burn has singed my tippers into charcoal. Nothing more than a flash. A light of electricity from the atmosphere. A spark. A jolt of power, useless to me, singing my flesh. Just another spring season. The grass should grow green again.

@

I have a new nest in my split. A family of birds. To them I have a purpose. It is not the wish. How wishes work is not theirs to be had. I know my wish, I have found that purpose. That purpose has come to me as soon as it has become dormant and restless.
Deep. Dark. Tunneled into the clay. My purpose is fear. It holds itself tight in the hard clay in the depths of the earth. Twists and knots. Holds itself. Twist, twirl, wrap, pull, tug, knot, twist, knot, tug, twirl, and never let them pull it from the earth. My purpose can never be free, for I am a tree. A poet in a tree.

@

The ants come one by one. One by one. They come one by one. The ants they come one by one. There are dark brown ants. There are dark brown ants. They come one by one. One by one come the dark brown ants. And the ants they come. One by one, the dark brown ants come. One by one. They use the indentations of my bark as their thoroughfares. One by one. No horns to honk, no lights to bare. No stop signs, no need to yield. These children of the planet are as choreographed as a precisely designed machine. My lineage being their map, their intuition their pace. Life is our guide. Together we are alive to the native eye.

His eye.

Your eye.

Her eye.

The child's mind.

The third's eye of the mind's eye in the fortunes' flight through singularity.

I see you, said the mouse, but it was the ants that made him believe that I was a poet to be.

'

'

'

'

"What's your name?" the strange little man asked me.

"I don't have a name?"

"You're moving. Trees don't move," he lectures me.

"You seem a little short to know everything?"

"I know how to read," he gloats.

"That's important. And I guess, I do not."

"How do you move though?"

"They're ants. And the wind moves my leaves."

"Oh, I see. You don't move."

,

,

,

,

@

Empty nest. Two of the five baby birds fell from the nest to their death. The soil has just begun to absorb its nutrients. The rain that'll come in a few weeks will give me some of that good stuff. Osmosis. I'm depressed. Little man sucked the passion out of me. I was on a roll. Thought I had a good thing going last spring. Almost thought I was a wri…

@
'

'

'

'

"Hold still," the little man, now a foot taller says, laughing at his own joke as he places a hand on me.

"What do you want with me?"
"Call me a giver."

and he jabs a flathead screwdriver right into me. Between the bark and corner of flesh. He digs. Pain. The pain. Rips a piece of bark. Reveals my flesh to the air. Begins to scrape into me. Letters, the letters of the alphabet. It hurts. The ants have scattered. They have lost logic. They know only madness. For now, only madness and pain. A, B, C, D, E, F, G, H, I, J, K, L, M N O P Q R S T U V W X Y Z

"Now you can read."

,

,

,

,
@
Liar. I could do nothing of the thing. Scared I was. Scared with the letters of an alphabet that only caused more confusion than clarity to a tree. Hieroglyphics of a madman was all I can see, could see, should see. Time present, past. Where was time if time was in presently past?
The birds and the bees were gone for the winter and the snow was going to give me some solitude. A time for a poet I'd so love to be.
@
'

'

'

'

"How old are you?"

"That's a personal question."

"I could find out."

"You would have to maim me."

"Would you grow back?"

"Depends how well you cut my limb."

"The lighting stumped your growth?"

"Made me stronger."

"Gave you character."

,

,

,

,

@

Character? What gives a tree character? This has never been a consideration of mine until he had come around. Before the little man, I had been content with an existence mute of ego. Now, he has painted me with a design, given me a uniqueness, a quality that I obtained.

As a creature born of nature, born of chemistry, of factions, the intellectual construct that humans say, "All life is unique," is terribly misguided from our shoes. On the contrary. Life is a general copy. There are misbalances along the way, yet for the most part, the copy is a copy and copies quite nicely, and repeats well. Advancements in design come over long periods of time and throughout generations and not within one's own lifetime. A smooth, bumpy-less ride. What makes one unique is when lightning strikes.

@

'

'

'

'

"Stay the fuck away from me."

But the little man is approaching with a grin and a girl.

"I want you to meet someone," he says.
"I'd rather not."
"Come on, you'll like her. Abigail, this a tree."
"Hello, Abigail."
"Hello, tree?" she says to me with a question, "Is that what you'd like me to call you, Tree?"

"He doesn't have a name."

"That's weird, everyone has a name."
The little man then proceeded to kiss this Abigail on the neck. It tickled her. She enjoyed this. She fell back against me. I held still. Made sure she had leverage. Her hands braced herself against my bark. I could feel her fingertips. I could read, yes read her fingerprints, like the rings within my own flesh. And soon her flesh was pressed against me. Her entire body, but it did not matter, it was her fingers, his fingers, that I could read as they caressed my bark as they made love to each other again and again year after year, night after night moon after sunlight after day after fight after flight after . . .

'

'

'

'

@
Year
Yea
r
Yea r
Y

e

a

r

Y E A R

@

,

,

,

,

"I have one last thing to write," the little man said. He was old now. So very, very old. He had been wheeled up the hill to me. So very old.

"How old are you now, sir?"
"A young Nine-Hundred and Seventy Two," he said.
"Magnificent. You don't look any older than…"
"The day we met," he interrupted me.
"I was going to say, the morning, but if you recall it as the day, then we can both recall it as the day."
"I'm going to climb you now," he said.
"You're too old and fragile. If you fall you will surely die."
"Then you won't let me fall. You will do something with yourself for once in your life and if I slip, you will move and catch my fall."

"But I cannot move."
He ignored me. He had spikes. Spikes in his gloves. Spikes in the soles of his shoes. And with those spikes he began to climb me. He carried with him a hoist, a hoist of gear. Gear he would use once he reached the split of my burnt stem.

"What are you trying to prove?"
"Nothing. I need to start at the top, that is all."

,

,

,

,

My trunk is not as thick the higher he goes. He grows weary of the rest of the climb. He has stopped. All that time I was sure he would reach the top. He seemed so determined.

Stubborn. It was me that was too weak to hold him. "I'll have to start from here," he says unpacking a set of ropes from his baggage. "What have you got there, twine?" He straddles himself between the stretch of a thick arm of mine before resting the bag upon it. From the bag he pulls a small saw. Not so much a saw as much as a cheese slicer? He places it in his pocket and then begins to pop the bark from my arm. Once cleared, sore and with my under skin exposed to the crisp air, this small little man removes the slicer from his breast pocket and proceeds to slice a thin layer of my flesh, my wooden flesh off my thick arm reaching from my trunk. I bleed sap. He sweeps it clean and licks the sour bland taste of plant from the tip of his finger. My sap is not very flavorful. He continues to shave my skin, again and again. Thinner and thinner. Lower and lower. One branch at a time. 5 inches at a time. 5 inches by 3 .5 inches at a time. The perfect size for a sheet of paper. One page at a time. And when each was shaven it was pinned to a branch to dry. And when he tired, he slept for the hour and then he awoken, and he shaved again until he slept for yet another hour until he awoke again until he slept for an hour.

@

I tell you what. I will tell you what is most unusual about things that are unusual to usual things. The diamond eyes of a feline's stare that burn an icicle so cold it steams until it smokes and falls and stabs the night. And that is the personal pain, that voice of insatiable trains slithered through hills, caverns, rivers into streams that break into creaks and beds and nightmares of fidelity and ash, dusty bodies all around, every step of the way. Every step he'll take the ash will break away and he'll gasp more. Suffocating in the environment he has built for himself as he dreamt within the pile of shaved papers that were the body of me.

He jerks up in a frenzy, gasping for air. "My lord," he is

petrified, "I, I couldn't breathe. I was, dreaming, I couldn't breathe. So much ash and debris. Ash and debris," he says to who, me? But I am just shears of myself. I am not a singularity. No, I am a fool, I am more than me, I am us. I am multiples. And it is through the dream that he has come to understand there is more to be done. That he must continue his work. He must set fire to a pile of us. He must burn us to a pile of ash. A charcoal. A substance of usefulness upon ourselves. We still wonder why the terrible, horrible abuse at the hand of this small little, now ever so elderly man. Pheph! And he sets the pile of shredded tree meat to flame.

He doesn't exist.
He doesn't resist.
He doesn't possess the stress,
Needed to get through the pressure,
The timeless crushing,
Necessary to squeeze the remaining sap left in deep in the fine soft membranes of the paper that have yet to dry.

If he could reach that substance. If he could draw that from my gut, then he could collect the ash, the burnt remnants of us and mash us into a mold, a mold to be battered back into a hardened mass as it dries into a coal, a lead. If only he could draw the sap from our soul that he so viciously sheared and hung out to dry, and then with no remorse and raptured euphoria burned a number of us before our eyes.
'

'

'

What was this strange little elderly man thinking now? What was he to do now? Was there nothing he could conjure to complete his undertaking? Would he not consider my roots?

His breathing is labored. His heartbeat tired. His hands, restless, his feet terribly numb. "That's it," he says with a sudden burst of energy and triumph of things beyond his control, standing on his numbed feet, "I have been frugal for times such as these. There is no need to exhaust measures," he cracks his neck and begins to dig into the soil, "Waste not the knot."

,

,

,

"What is it?" asked the mouse.
"Not sure," said the mongoose.
"Should we pull it?" asked the mouse.
"Won't know unless we do," said the mongoose.
The mouse pulled the string from the hole in the wall.
The mongoose sat and watched the mouse pull the string across the room until he got to the other side. "Now what?" asked the mouse.
"Put it back," said the mongoose.
The mouse spent the rest of its life trying to put the string back in the little hole that was the exact circumference of the string itself.
@
Eight months have passed, and the strange little man has dug along a single root of mine for a good 55 yards. I have thinned down to a diameter of 3 inches and if the old man gets his sixty winks, he thinks with the wiggle he's got on it now, he'll finally get the root to release and set it free from the soil it has been holding onto for dear life.

-    -   -   -   --   --   -- -- --

- "Let's do this," and with that he leaps to his numbed feet and wiggles and wiggles and wiggles my root free from the soil, falling backwards onto the ground himself where he fumbles around hugging the root and laughing to himself, "Oh the joy, oh the joy!" – Yes. Yes, oh the joy of digging a 60-yard root free from the soil. Oh, the joy.

dug . dug . dug he dug . dug . dug . oh the joy .

@

The strange little man has lifted the root upside up, upside down, upside right, upside left. He's turned it the side, turned it to the poles. He's done the this and the that to get the grip of graps, the graps of grips to twist and twirl the root. Twirl the twist. Twirl the twine. Twist and tweak. Twiggle and tweak. Twist and twarrle. Twarrle and twist the sap a drip, drip, drip upon the pile of ash. A drip a drip upon the pile of ash. A dust poof, smokes into the air from the drip of drop of sap into the boof of ash. The drips and drops, sapping and slopping together. No more poofs. The ooze pushes down upon itself. Rolling over the ash. A lava. A cool, maple lava rolling over the ash of its own burnt meat. And soon after hours of twists and twirls, and winks upon winks, the strange little man will knead the sap and ash with his bare hands. Once fully kneaded, the strange elderly little man rolls the mash into a series of thick dowels. Dowels after dowels. Stacking them upon each other. Dowels upon dowels. Sap ash dowels baking in the sun. For weeks he watched patiently as the sap ash dowels dried and hardened in the sun. In the meantime, he stacked the rest of us into piles with stones upon the top to prevent the wind from blowing us into oblivion. He has been quiet since he had sung his song of joy. As if he has either lost his voice completely, or silently vowed to no longer speak to us. We still prayed for a day we all could live a life of great purpose.
@

He has taken a dowel from the top of a pile. It seems solid, dry. He removes a stone from one of the paper piles and takes a single sheet of us from that pile.

There is a moment where he does nothing more.

He places me onto my stump. I can see him look down right

at me. He has great passion in his eyes. Although the skin around his eyes is so very wrinkled and loose, I can still make out that he is very much alive in his dying years. He licks the sharpened tip of the sap ash dowel, "You taste sour, my friend," he says to me, and begins to scratch the sharp tip along my skin. . . and because a long time ago he once taught me how to read, I can read what he is scratching and it reads, "If you've ever had a Mom, you'd understand that you mean the world to them, or not."

And as a tree I have to wonder, don't we all have the same mother?

ABOUT THE AUTHOR

Tzvi Peckar the Third is a native-born Northern Californian who has rested his head in Manhattan, Los Angeles, & the San Francisco North Bay Area, along with extended stints upon Puerto Rico, and abroad. An observer, a researcher, a wanderer, self-proclaimed scuttlebutt, and extreme culturalist, Peckar had spent his young adult life on the cutting edge of society, celebrating the best of its art, music, film, and strangeness. His first published work were the psychedelically charged series, "Tzvi's Trees: Short Stories About Weed," followed by his self-published novels Mini Thins, and UNO. His notoriety is nothing, save for his proximity to his illegitimate-identical twin brother cult filmmaker Tawd b. Dorenfeld, best known for The Anna Cabrini Chronicles.

Tzvi continues to live in a state of bliss with his wife, dogs, & cats in Detroit.